Beneath the
Blue Dusk and the Sea

Short Stories by

Wendy Rathbone

**Beneath the Blue Dusk and the Sea - Copyright ©
2014 by Wendy Rathbone and Eye Scry Publications.**

A publication by:
Eye Scry Publications
http://www.eyescrypublications.com

ISBN 13 # 978-0989693899
TITLE: Beneath the Blue Dusk and the Sea
Author: Wendy Rathbone

A young man meets two mer-people from the sea; through future nuclear destruction, two pucks make their way home to elfland; a young girl at the end of the world waits for new spring; a trapped jinn writes an open letter online; while care-taking a crippled "thing" a young man finds his heart; two men stumble into another dimension; in a future where everyone is beautiful, the one guy who is ugly tells his story; space exploration has become a scripted soap opera until someone tampers with the script...

For Della

Beneath the
Blue Dusk and the Sea

Table of Contents

Beneath the Blue Dusk and the Sea

There's a girl on the sea-cliff walking, and the salt wind washes up through the leaves tangling the trees, jostling against my house. The flavor of the day is raspberry, a reeling plum sky, fantastic blue/green clouds masking the tawny sun as it goes down and down against the edges of the dark eastern day. The sea wind is an arrow that always finds its mark. I can hear it scrabbling on the roof, whining. It will find me again eventually, even if it takes a lifetime.

In the meantime, I watch it wake the girl's hair, long and bronze, and tease the drooping blue sleeves of her coat, the long skirt of it fighting at her legs to be a sail on a ship, to be free.

A tall, black dog follows behind her on this afternoon walk. Running. Exploring. But never straying more than a dozen yards away, always circling back to her, always letting her lead.

Even though it's been fifty years, I know her. Seaweed eyes and a sea-foam kiss. Parched from land and adrift at sea.

They've come back for me.

*

The storm flashes suddenly, frightening even the sky itself until it cracks. The sea leaps, wild.

Fifty years ago…and it's just like yesterday.

I am standing at the top of the cliff with my pitchfork trying to look menacing. It is, after all, my job.

You see, the kids often cut across the orchard after school, short-cuts to home perhaps, or just up to mischief. My master thinks they're stealing fruit. He puts up 'NO TRESPASSING' signs. They're not entirely effective, so he's hired me. "Chase 'em off, Jack!" he yells from his porch. I keep the weeds down and do general landscaping. And I scare the kids away. Ravens and gulls, too.

The pay is decent. I can wear old, patched clothes to work…not have to worry about a suit and tie. I can grow my bangs long and dark. I can shave every other day.

This day the weather is untamed, frenzied, too cold even for kids. It's so strong it is like an ocean of itself, buffeting, twisting around my legs like a school of lampreys. For days now, the sea has been in an angry mood, tossing up mermaid's hair in windrows on the sand, breaking higher and higher against the bluffs. Staring down at its cauldron depths, the monster approaches.

In this weather, I get little work done. The trees hunch into themselves. The fruit is fall-withered. The gulls hide. The pumpkins in their patches huddle into the earth.

The master is warm and fast in his big house, sitting by a fire no doubt, reading his professorial books with his half-moon glasses in his long red robe. And here I am, out in this godforsaken mass riot of the end of the world, looking for errant kids who know better, who are inside sitting at kitchen tables with big mugs of hot chocolate and reading colorful comic books. Little Tommy Thumb ain't hiding in the ditch today. No one is.

If I cut out of work early, who would notice?

It's ridiculous, actually, me standing in a hurricane with a stupid pitchfork like some young Pa Kettle, or pathetic Poseidon, or flimsy scarebird about to be rassled to pieces by a bastard nor'easter.

Yeah. And no. Time to freakin' clock out.

I turn for one last look. It is, truthfully, a prickly sight. The tides mug each other right and left. Salt spray mists and stings. Beyond, like some sick, black beast, the waters fold and swell, churning, hurtling, enraged. The sky is black on darker black, rolling and broken.

I've seen a few men pissed off that bad before. Their eyes glowing red for the kill.

8

Out loud I mutter, "It's cool, dude. I'm going. I'm going."

Unappeased, a sudden gust throttles me. Cursing, I keep my balance and turn but another one follows, stronger, as if it wants to fight. Then another and another. My hat flies away. I am mobbed. I go down hard on my knees. I scrabble for the dropped pitchfork, grab the wooden handle, rake the tines in the sandy earth. But now it's as if inhuman hands have hold of my ankles. The pitchfork drags, not holding my weight. The handle breaks.

Grabbing at fleeing air, I tumble off the cliff.

As if I am made of nothing but straw, the wind kites me.

*

I bob up from the dark water coughing silt. As soon as my mouth is clear, the sea smacks me and fills me up again. I choke. How'd I get here? I think I must be dreaming. I'm drowning. Acid fills my nose and throat. Murk and death. It's all I see.

Twisted. Tossed. Turned and turned again. Down and up. Eely hands on my ankles pull, again pull. My last heartbeat isn't even a tap perceived beyond the loud ocean drum in my ears.

*

My master's house might be considered by some to be ornate, rich, mansion-ish. It's big. Yes. But I've seen bigger.

Professor. Purveyor of anecdotes, tidbits, useless things he calls knowledge. Collector. He hoards like a nested dragon. On a two-year sabbatical from the college, he rarely leaves his 'cottage' by the sea.

Extreme bookcases line the walls of his living room and study. What space isn't taken up by books, and isn't windows, is filled with odd pictures, woodcuts, pieces of art from far-off lands, butterfly boxes where the colorful critters are pinned eternally to black, velvet-smothered cardboard. Knick-knacks abound on every surface drawing dust. Weird shells, rocks, gourds, bird nests, candle ends. Little carved figures that look like gnomes, or fairies, or fish. An ancient set of Russian dolls. Ash trays, wood boxes, the occasional dead spider. Lining one wall near the top of the ceiling are grimacing, African masks. In a dark corner, old skin drums. It is a cave of eccentricity. A swap meet from Hell.

I've been inside only a few times. Usually he pays me as I stand on the porch at his door. Once a week. Cash. But sometimes, if the wind is blowing exceptionally strong, or it's raining, he invites me in.

There is just too much to see at one glance. I can't help it. My eyes wander over everything. Some of the book spines are so old I cannot read the titles, but some stand out. He's got, it seems, all of Shakespeare. Myths. Legends. Science. Darwin's "On the Origin of Species" stands out. He sees me looking and walks over to the shelf, takes it down.

"Darwin," he says. "Do you know who he is?"

I glance aside to keep from rolling my eyes. I am college educated, but I always omit that from my applications because with the types of jobs I prefer to take these days it only over-qualifies me.

I say nothing, but I do nod.

"It's a first edition."

My eyebrows rise at that.

He shrugs as if it's nothing. "E-Bay," he mumbles, and puts it back.

Sometimes I feel as if I'm guarding against something more than just two-bit kid thieves. Even when there's nothing left for me to do, my master wants me there seven to five inspecting the fences, keeping an eye out.

Once I said to him, "Kids run about at night, too, you know."

10

He replied, turning away, "They don't come at night." And the way he said the word "they" made me suddenly doubt he was talking about kids at all.

Rain hails against the windows. His hearth gutters. He has a decanter and a flask on an oak table by his puffy leather chair. He does not ask me to sit. He does not offer me a drink. I stand patiently on an old, Chinese rug and try not to drip on it.

He has lost interest in me immediately, as if his attention is always elsewhere. But he does remember to fetch my pay. He puts it in my hand, then says, "Tomorrow, seven sharp."

As if being late would wreck his world.

*

I am pulled and scoured and lost. Salt-filled. Frozen. Nothing but brine in my lungs and eyes and ears. All I can hear is a giant roar that never stops. The allure of pure blackness. It's killing me over and over.

Then, incredibly, through death and freezing dark and no identity, I see a face as lovely as a star, bronze and glowing, eyes like slits of flame. It's floating in front of me as if disembodied, but then I feel something surround me, slick and strong, like a naked muscle wrapping my waist. Impossibly, I hear a voice, distant, vibrating, pitched like the cry of a gull. "Breathe. Breathe." Something sponge-soft and squirming touches my lips. I retch. I choke. And then there's air.

Still the sick sea tosses me. But within it something holds me firm. Encases me. Bubbles against my mouth with life. It seems there are two things holding me now, one before me, one behind. Four arms. Or tentacles. Or god knows what. And that thickness, slippery and strong, still wraps my lower torso like a snake. The slamming sea gentles as they keep me in their grip.

11

Still, I am being held down. Down. But I can feel again. It's not so cold. Whatever holds me transfers a strange kind of kindling fire to my body. I realize my clothes have been long ago ripped away, sea-taken.

We float. I think I fall asleep.

*

My master rarely leaves his house. He has food and other packages delivered. He eschews all social invitations. He never even takes walks along the beach.

I understand a bit about agoraphobia. Anxiety. Depression. Stress. But this guy exhibits none of these symptoms. It's more like he's hiding. Or hiding something.

I want to get inside his house alone. I need to.

But he's always there. Always.

*

Sand rasps against my hip and thigh, scrapes my shoulder, trickles to a fine itch through my hair. I am no longer being shredded, ripped, slashed. The world is a little more steady now. Although everything is still past dark.

My first thought: How am I alive?

Then I feel movement against my back and something settles on my chest, round and warm, smelling of sea-winds and bitter ale. No, the bitterness is coming from behind. The sweetness is in front.

I can see only shadows in this gloom, but I feel them now. The same two from the clashing waves. We three are salt-bashed, water-crushed but blessedly washed ashore.

How are we alive?

The gull-voice erupts suddenly, swirling around us in a strangely quiet air. "We are alive. You have yet to be saved, Jack."

"What?" My voice is dust.

12

Then from behind, low, melodic, "We have a price."

"What?" I try to move. They hold me tight, close as we were in the water, closer...until I gasp.

"You are not yet home. And this is not your beach," he says, for there can be no doubt now, as he prods me, that whatever it is behind me is male.

The sweet essence in front of me lifts her head from my chest. "Jack."

"How do you know my name?"

"We know who you are. It's why we brought you here."

"Here?"

"Undersea," the male responds.

"To our eternal dawn," the female adds.

"In the season we call umber," he says.

"No light ever here," she says.

He whispers in my ear. "We live in the land of Neverlight."

This must be my death-rattle. My last hallucination. My afterlife dream. Because none of this can be.

"Think again," he says and I feel his knee against my leg. Knee?

In front of me, the "girl" is smooth, supple and strange. Her body seems to end at her waist. The rest of her, wrapped now about my knees and ankles, is a thick, long muscle like a tail. She is not human.

But the male? He doesn't end at the waist. In fact, he is all-too crudely human, firm arms locked about me, that knee against the back of my thigh.

The mind is a funny thing...that I would dream this.

The girl lifts her head, kisses me. I can feel her soft hair paint my jaw and neck. "Not a dream." Her golden voice. Her breath like fresh, sweet rain on my face.

*

He opens the door. A frown feeds the crease between his graying eyebrows. He looks as if I have just interrupted him at something important. Annoyed.

Yes, this man is definitely hiding. This wise professor. This artifact collector. My master.

But then he looks at me, focus re-doubled. Up and down. Taking me in. Noticing. I've combed my hair to the side. I've shaved. I smile and shrug. "Yeah," I reply to the unspoken question in his eyes. "It's a new suit. I saved up for it."

"But you don't need that for the work you do here...," voice muffled by confused distraction.

I lift my left hand which holds the wicker handle of a tawny basket. Within I have arranged the choicest apples I could find from his withered orchard. I hold it out to him. "I thought you might want to have these. They were what survived the storm."

Tentative, he reaches out, palm curving on the handle, and takes it from me. "Thank you. I wasn't expecting..."

"I know," I interrupt. I look past his shoulder at the copper-shadowed depths of his home. He's watching me closely. Curious.

Good.

Finally, he sighs, a weak, deflated sound. "Would you like to come in?"

"Why yes, thank you."

He takes the basket and puts it on a table by a couch that faces the fire. He never uses the couch that I have seen. Always the chair. I go to the basket, lift an apple out. "You should try one. They're very sweet."

"No," he replies, almost as if dismissing me. "You go ahead."

I put the apple to my lips.

He turns and watches me. I crunch the juicy bite, nod and smile.

"You're a very strange man, Jack," he says.

14

Taken aback, I glance aside. "I am?" In all this time, he has never even tried to get to know me.

"Well, you have to admit, you haven't been very friendly before."

"Never get the chance. You hide here, you know."

He smiles when I say that. "Yeah, I guess I do."

"What's your secret?"

"You think I have a secret?"

"Yeah, I do."

His eyes suddenly give off a strange sparkle. "Don't we all?"

I take a deep breath, then take another bite of my apple. I turn away and start pacing back and forth along his bookshelves, gently touching the spines as I go. Reverently petting the nesting dolls. Stirring the dead spider in a giant, up-turned scallop shell. "Where did you get all this stuff?"

"I collect things," he replies.

"It's wonderful. I love old things. Rare things."

"It's a passion of mine," he offers. "Finding one of a kind items for a good price. I can't afford Monets or van Goghs, but some things make their way to me, things I discover, and it's like buried treasure lost, then found."

"Nice hobby."

"Yeah…"

"So what would you say in all your stuff would be your favorite item? The rarest? That Darwin book, maybe?"

He shakes his head.

"Not telling?" I ask.

He smiles and it's like a kid at Christmas. Yes, he has a secret. A big one.

His face cannot conceal his glee even if he tried. "Why would you care anyway, Jack?"

"How long have I worked for you?"

"Two years."

"It's hard not to wonder."

"Fair enough," he says. "But no, I don't think I would like to say."

"Okay, okay." My smile is friendly. "But I had to try." But he is taken. I can see it. When I clean up, I clean up nice. I have a quality that makes people look twice. He motions to the couch. "Sit. Since you came…and brought food, we can chat at least."

"I'd like that."

*

"We have a price," the man behind me says, gripping tight. And now I know, it is a man, even if he is stronger than any I have ever known and strangely sea-worthy, able to survive even the most furious squalls, able to catch me at my drowning with his mermaid girlfriend and bring me here.

"So for now I am dead?" I can feel my body, cold and shaking. I have a sensation of breath, or how could I even speak?

The girl answers. "Best to say not quite alive."

The air smells of brine, acid, salt. The sting in my nose, the headache…I've either drowned or have the flu. I look up. The sky is like no sky I've ever seen. It pulses and undulates like a black, liquid thing. The sound inside it is like a rush of wind. There are no stars.

No light. 'Undersea,' he had said when I asked where we were.

The sand beneath my quivering body is sharp and soft and fine and gritty all at the same time. Made up of a million rocks and bones and shells all whittled down over millions of years to this fine grain. Finally, I ask, "Who are you people?"

They answer in turn. "Cayia." "Nereid." "Siren." "Selkie."

Unlucky omens, all.

"But you're human," I say, referring to the man at my back.

"A temporary state at great inconvenience," he replies.

I am thirsty and tired and sick. They are not nursemaids. They don't offer me a hearth or bed or meal. They don't give me clothing or coffee or kind words. Instead, as I lie there trying to decide if I am dreaming or dead, they give me their story and their deal.

*

"I heard a rumor about you," I say when the older man finally offers some hot tea to go with the cold of the day, of his distant dark eyes.

"Me?" He laughs, waving me off. The firelight quivers around the room and over his face making his half-glasses look like two caught moons. "I've only ever taught at the college. And my students were always off-limits...not by law but my own choice."

"No, nothing like that."

"I'm an eccentric, aging man, nothing else."

"Still...your collection..."

I see it happen almost immediately, the wary shutting down, a dullness in his gaze, mistrust, suspicion.

Quickly, I say, "Hey, I'm not trying to pry. But you collect with no idea of ever showing off what you win? For example, museums..."

"You don't work for any museum," he interrupted.

I shake my head. "Of course not."

His eyes squint. Voice hard, "Get to the point."

Keeping my own voice relaxed, I say, "I know someone. He's a buyer looking for something very very rare. He asked me to ask. Maybe you have it, maybe you don't, but..."

Abrupt. "Nothing I own is for sale."

"But you haven't even heard what he's looking for. Or the price."

"I don't care. I have nothing for sale. Nothing."

I smile. "Okay, then. Couldn't hurt to ask, right?"

He relaxes slightly when I let up. He lets out a heavy breath. I reach for another apple. "You should try these...so sweet."

Eying me for a moment, he finally relents. "Yes, all right."

I hand him the best-looking one of the bunch. As he eats it, his eyes droop. Slowly, he falls to sleep.

*

We seal the deal. A bond is formed to ensure my loyalty; their magic must become a part of me. Her kiss of foam and cream. His salty power at my back.

From somewhere a glow ignites the air, soft as pre-dawn...or maybe my eyes are adjusting. I can see the two of them. His hair is thick and long and oak brown as he leans into me. She is all bronze, her hair so long it becomes lost past her waist. Her face is like a white oval, delicate but severe, the cheeks sharp, the chin a point. His face is dark and mesmerizing, square and old, yet he looks young as a boy...the oldness is shown only by the strength in him, and the weathered leathery hardness of his chestnut skin. His eyes are blue as paradise. Hers are the shade of green you might see alcoved behind a waterfall where the grass is never trod. She is fresh as spring. He is of the north.

Her thick-muscled tail unwinds itself from me, dolphin pale; it flaps upon the sand. At first I think the glitter I see upon it is just the sand but then I realize they are fine, tiny scales, glistening gold to green. The beauty of it stuns me. The scales seem to flick side to side in rows, then slowly come apart, undoing themselves, shedding to the side like sand, and underneath...two slippery, pale legs.

I gasp as they spread for me and her arms come over my shoulders.

18

The demon-man – her husband? -- grabs me harder from behind.

"Just so you never forget you are ours." I can't tell which one of them speaks. The voice is only in my head now, alive and vibrant.

The girl mounts me and if I thought I was overwhelmed by that I realize my shock is only a fraction of what I feel when they both grab me hard from front, from behind. Everything is wet and hot. He is rough and bold, holding me there. His strong, slick arms close about my chest. He whispers steamy against my ear, raspy, "Find my skin."

Her hands comb through my hair. The two seem to possess me until I toss my head back, cry out my promise to them. He cups my chin. His kiss is a tang of tide, storm-scented, corruption of winds beyond known time. There is then, planted within me, the threat of returning, wilding sea, my drowning, my obliteration if I fail.

For the promise of fifty more years on land, a lifetime really, I must return his life. To him. To them. They tell me exactly where to find it. Seal-skin. Dolphin-skin. Mer-male skin.

A stolen soul. Now they want it back.

When my fifty years are up, they will return.

*

My master sleeps.

As soon as I'm sure he is "out," I jump up and start my search. The house is large but it doesn't take long. He doesn't hide things. Why should he? He lives alone. No one ever comes to visit. Except me.

Upstairs I enter the master bedroom. It is a tapestry-clad, ornate, darkened room, but the prize possession I seek is immediately apparent. It glitters upon the wall-space over the headboard, fine-scaled and gently finned, shimmering gold-green, the rarest tapestry of them all. It measures about 5 X 3 feet, and is fitted with a metal clip that pierces through one edge. I grimace to see that, but whatever shape the skin is in, he wants it back.

I have to stand on the bed to take it down. It feels like silk and sequins in my hands, light and airy, smooth and dry.

Once he gets it back, he will no longer be stuck in his human form. By day he'll be able to take any shape until dusk when these beings automatically revert back to their water-selves. Even without his skin, stuck in human form, he'd been cursed to go to the water at night, remain there in his salty habitat until morning. Or die.

This was the reason my master needed a full-time, daylight scare-guard. So they'd never be able to take it back. I look down at the skin, fold it gently, then drape it over my arm.

As I turn, still standing on the bed, the old man walks in, unsteady, half-drunk...but awake. I have underestimated the potency of what I gave him in the apple. He has a small revolver and he's aiming straight at me.

"Put it back."

I drop the skin and it falls lightly, softly to the bedspread. I've already died one too many times this week. I open my hands to my sides. "Don't shoot."

"Who hired you?" He's shaking, but he's got a firm grip on that gun.

"You did."

"Not as my own thief!"

I nod. While I was Undersea, they both whispered their names, complex series of sounds and cries and songs I can barely remember. "I cannot pronounce his name."

"I will call the police and you'll be arrested."

"But this is not yours to keep," I reply.

"They won't care or understand any of that. I have the bill of sale. That's all that matters!"

"All that matters? So you know what this is?"

20

"It's the best, most wonderful thing I've ever owned. It sends me to magical lands. It keeps me. It holds me. Immortal. You touched it. Surely you felt the pleasure..."

"But it belongs to someone who without it can't be who he is, can't be whole!"

"A myth!"

"You hired me to guard against a myth?"

"It's mine now. I won't give it up!"

"You tricked him. Or whoever sold it to you did! Doesn't that mean anything?"

His eyes go hazy and dark. His voice hard as stone. "No."

I jump off the bed and reach for the skin.

"Don't!"

"I'm taking it. Otherwise you'll have to shoot me." I hold the skin tight to my chest.

It never occurred to me my master could really kill. But even drugged as he is, my challenge seems far too easy for him to dismiss. He lifts the revolver and pulls the trigger.

I feel very little. In fact, for a moment I think he has missed. Then a warmth, like a small burn, permeates my right shoulder. My mouth opens in shock just as another shot goes off. My body jerks. This time I see blood well at my side.

Fifty years, they had said. Well, it looks as if they lied. I feel myself start to fall, the floor coming up way too fast. My master walks over to me, looking down at me now. He holds the gun pointed at my face. "It is the allure of the All," he says quietly. "Do you realize that skin is immortal?"

I look at it, still clutched in my hand. When he shoots me again, I am faster. I lift the skin over my face. The bullet repels off it. I hear something hard hit the floor. When I sit up to see what has happened, my master lies beside me, silent. Blood wells from a bullet wound in his forehead and drips slowly into his hair.

I look down at the skin in my hands. The bullet had ricocheted off its immortal strength.

Injured, bleeding, I leave the house. The outside is a dark tempest of dizzying gravity and night as I stumble in a fever from my blood-loss. The sea roars. I did not kill my master, but the authorities will not automatically believe that. There will be questions I cannot answer. My presence there will guarantee my guilt.

I run.

Down the cliff steps. Away from the top-land onto damp sand, tripping over seaweed piles, small dunes and weeds.

The tide moves like a manic creature, undulating, sensitive. In it, two figures float. As I fall weakly to my knees at the edge of the water, the one with the legs comes forward. He takes the skin from my hands, wraps it about himself. He says, almost shouting over the sound of the waves, "A deal is a promise, too! I thank you!" And touches my forehead with wet, slippery hands, combing tightly through my tangled hair. Already the skin is forming around him, phosphor and mica, creating the tail, but still he does not leave. He kneels before me, tears the buttons of my dress shirt, and sticks his hand inside. His palm caresses my shoulder, stinging, then my side. The pain recedes.

When he withdraws, his hand is dyed black with my blood. Two misshapen metal slugs lie wet and red in his palm. Then he touches the side of my face with the very tips of his icy fingers. "Jack," he says. "Live well."

Within one blink, they are both off, glistening bodies sliding like light vanishing into the dark, night sea.

*

I never intended to become like my master. Never. But there are several reasons I went into hiding and lived the eccentric life of a shut-in.

The first: The police in that area staged a wide-ranging man-hunt for me. It was not easy to elude them, and even years later I remain in a half-paranoid state that cops could come pounding at my door at any moment and cuff me and take me away.

The second: What the selkies didn't tell me was that not only would I have fifty years of health-filled life, but I would also never age. That small detail gets noticed.

For years I have watched the sea. I have two telescopes, three sets of binoculars, and an old telescoping spyglass. I've seen dolphins play in the white-caps, whales migrating and spraying their breaths into the air, gulls playing, pelicans diving, pleasure boats, destroyers, swimmers, surfers, even a mild shark or two. But never in all these fifty years did I spy the selkies. Not once, even in my dreams.

Now I watch her on the bluing cliffs, the sky like the sea behind her, like the liquid rafters of her native land, and the wind curls about her curious and questing, perhaps noticing she is out of place.

The black dog moves beyond the grace of its shape.

I didn't think, when the time came, they'd arrive like this. I thought I'd see them, pale and mysterious figures on the waves, beckoning, or as sea-wraiths flooding my home with salt water in the middle of the day and stealing me away.

As the edge of the pink sun's disk touches the surface of the turquoise land, I walk out onto my porch.

The girl looks up. The dog stops, sniffs, and turns my way.

As they come for me, I can already feel their minds inside me, their thoughts, their world of floating castles in murk-drowned depths. I can see the wild sea opening. Weeping, I hear myself call a name I never remembered and cannot pronounce. My lips sting with salt. Shedding the past, I move forward. Already I can see the starless underland. I am moving toward them and into their liquid dark arms.

୧ৡৡ

Under The World

where the water blues to gray-driven ink
flowing toward starless north
where the many-voiced wind
goes schizophrenic
where betrayal begins and ends
with self
or Charon
or whoever there is to blame
where the river bottom falls
into a submerged garden
of black sea-flowers
    shadows swim
in carbon foam
along the wrecks and hulks
of antimatter ships
    they lounge
in secret shoals, tributaries and brooks
channeling midnight
dark-finned, slim and shining
    mermen of the river Styx

Sooth and Sull: A Story For A Rainy Day

The wind rippled oddly red because of the fires.

Distant castles of smoke.

Ravens of ash.

Before the bomb, Sullivan and I were counting leaves. The apple-gold. The russet. All the dead browns. Twenty two million seventeen thousand and thirty three. We had been focused. At it for weeks.

Now the sylvan wood ran black in the blood-breeze. We could smell the dying oaks, the harsh lessons of withered air.

The wizard trees that did not burn lived on but had nothing to say.

I had a talisman that was a star. Eccentric. Shy.

Sullivan's was a black lace glove like spider webbing. He could wear it always, but mine was gone for now. I could not find it in all those glazed-garnet skies.

"Share mine," Sull said. We twined our hands together inside the stretched material.

That night we'd also lost the moon. Lace was all we had left.

Well, in truth, we still had our striped socks, our fangs, our cliffs of hair.

And of course we had each other.

Awhile back the Thunder-lord had de-winged us. Sull had only wanted to be bigger. I had asked for a human heart.

It was all more complicated than that, as politics and law-breaking always is, but exile claimed our fate. It was how we met.

I was from the Sutherlands, tall and long. Sull, who was a Northman called me Sooth. He was a "little man" who, standing on his toes, barely reached my waist.

We are of the same race, both pucks, but different lands had shaped us. Humans call us goblins or hobs. But actually we call ourselves sylphs and the females of our kind are dryads. No sylph had seen a dryad in millennia and none knew why. They vanished long ago.

The bomb had wrecked the wood too well. We had been long away from home. Exile was eternal. But all we could think to do was return to Upper Gate, a wrought-iron double door patterned in a hundred-weave knot suspended by two white-marble crumbling columns.

The gate led under the world. It stood alone on a hill made of rock-patched land. Though its knot was tangle-locked against us, we both still had the urge to return. There was no straight way to get to it. The path to the gate was round-about. And so we had to figure it out.

We had not seen home, southern or northern, for over a hundred years.

The bomb changed everything.

It began to snow ash. Fine silver. Iridescent gray. A dusk and chill scent.

"Sooth, the night may never end."

"I know."

We shook the chary swirls from our hair as we walked. I had borrowed a black trench with tails from a camper years ago. I paid him with a hand-knit scarf of wool I'd carded from Suffolk sheep. So much ash. The coat turned white. We looked bearded. Old. But we truly never aged. Sull appeared youthful with a full head of black spirals steering all directions in the air. I had brown braids that folded over my left shoulder. I kept them banded.

But we could not escape the ash. It was everywhere.

Without sun, the wind dressed cold. We slept curled about each other for warmth, Sull's head to my chest, my face in his hair. The grieving trees bowed over us.

Whenever nature changed a course we pucks would feel unusual aches and tiredness in our bones. We never die, but we get cravings to go to earth and rest a century or two. Loam and roots and sediment call us to their beds.

But the greater pull right now was Upper Gate.

We woke in a white drift of silt. Walked on. The fairy rings were all gone. We couldn't use them for easier passage. Trees swooned. The wind went violet. It was a great shadow without a mind.

We came upon a little town with backwoods arbors, picket-fenced. Sull found an old swing in a dead tree and played upon it, rocking. Swings were emblems of joy to us. De-winged, we used them to re-mount the sky. Swings were their own paths in a world of so much highway and cars. Today he said it made him sick.

In a ginger-house we found old food, no good, but comfortable pillows and new clothes. We were not thieves so for everything we took we left little piles of emeralds and rubies even though the family had long fled. Sull fell in love with a purple jacket. It made him smile, was meant to be. I took candles, and a pretty plastic pony with pink hair. I hung it from my collar on a string.

In a king four-poster bed we fell to sleep again and dreamed of the broken wind. Outside the world turned. It was just a darker color.

We woke and moved on, looking for the short-cuts, time passages, finding none.

We came to torn cities that scraped the tortured, oily sky. Ashen streets gleamed with ice from the distant lights of survivors' torches. And from glimmers of my own swaying candled lamp.

Sull found the body of a child in the road. He held her for an hour. When he finally let her down he placed a five-lobed leaf upon her mouth. My lantern reflected in the shiny lines upon his face.

I had no human heart, but I held his hand.

The trick of the earthly puck is this: to make the world's luck. The bomb re-set a lot of things. It was going to take a long time for us to fix the flaw.

More cities. A dance macabre. The carnivale gone wrong. Buildings and statues, empty-eyed, watched us pass them by. Boardwalks, alleys, railroads all led otherwhere. But we needed otherwhen for our pilgrimage to Upper Gate. We needed fireflies and broom factories. Satyr-glens and mermaid coves. I missed my talisman, the star.

One day a raven called from atop a split gazebo. "Dreary daring day," it said.

"The same down here," Sull replied.

With rain had come the scent of nether-seas, and fog. The road was salt and shale now. We had hoped we were getting close. But we could not see. The distance was all white leading to green-dark agate skies.

The raven's black eye moved side to side and preened us with his gaze. "Diving deep, dire."

"Can you see from your high seat," Sull called, "if we are close to Upper Gate?"

"Direction death. Direction dog. Direction dream."

"Which is it, kind sir?"

And it was true, what Sull said. Despite horror yarns and ballads and old folk tales, all ravens were a kindly sort.

"Domain," said the raven. "Down." His head bent; the bead-eye fixed upon where he perched.

We looked where he tilted and saw the fog within the skeleton framework of the arches, misting up the gazebo steps.

We followed the haze, stepped underneath the quivering lattices and the mostly missing roof. I lost sight of Sull so fast I spun in place and braced myself to fall. I felt my coattail tugged and tripped out onto vast dead lawns of dandelions bent and black-singed.

"It was only one more step," Sull reprimanded.

"I got lost."

28

"You don't say."

He kicked his leg, pointing with his pointy shoe. "There."

I saw it in the clearer air, atop a slag-rock knoll, a black knotted drawing on the pale page of sky. An iron puzzle five stories high. Chipped and scarred, two marble columns framed it on each side. It looked like a leftover relic from an era of giants, curved and spiked at the peak where it steepled frigid earth-winds. You could hear the echoes beyond it. You could smell the honeyed land.

Upper Gate.

From our vantage, it appeared to lead nowhere. On the other side of the gate was no framed or fenced estate, no castles, no brighter world. Just more rock on rock. More empty hills and fields.

It was a trick. The gate hid so much more.

We made our way past clumps of dirt and stone to stand before the entrance to our olden world.

Sull said, "Well, here we are," and kicked one of the iron legs. It clanged once, a low moan.

I touched my fingertips to an edge of knot bigger than my hand. They burned as if I'd reached for ice.

Sull yelled, "Hello!"

The wind had voices in it, that was all.

"I came out this way," I said.

"Me, too."

"I never tried to get back in. The gate shut. It was a new full world."

"Yeah. But you know me. I make friends wherever I go."

It was true. I smiled. It was also true he'd chosen me.

Sull continued. "I flirted with the gatekeeper. I gave him two blue feathers and a rook. He collects rooks, you know."

"I didn't know."

"That's because you never plan ahead. Hey, Fantie. Fantie!" He banged the gate-leg again causing a dim bell sound. "It's Sullivan. Open up! I have more rooks from chess sets you have never seen. I've been saving them just for you."

The metal design of the knot began to move. Slowly the tangled iron began to unravel and separate in the middle. The brittle sound of owls came, something screeching, something breaking. Nails scraping bone.

Slowly the gigantic gate parted down the front and two sides swung inward with a final aching shriek.

Rain. Tea. Lava. Honey.

Tulip. Powder. Apple. Wick.

Sun. Elm. Moss. Snow.

Cloaks and hinged lanterns and slender fall moons.

The rich stress of stars. The wine of marble graves. Root and leaf. Wafts of earthen mortals who have wandered into traps. The beeswax air. The merry emerald-eyed walls. Sips of time. Wedges of escaping green. Banished beauty frothing forth.

Two worlds combined for a moment in transition. Clouds were punctured in multi-season assaults.

Through the open gate, the human world sucked on all this richness in starved frenetic fury. There was an endless supply yet still Sullivan said, "Hurry!"

But like Sull's depthless pockets from which he pulled one treasure after another, real fairy magic never ran out. Never died. There was no hurry.

The gate could stay ajar and let things out, but within there'd still be more new Januaries and Augusts, more pinecones and peaches and nebulae.

Already the outside sky hinted at a blushing day. But just as the gate let things out it could also let things in we pucks might never want. So it was kept mostly locked and closed.

"Sooth, come on!" Sull called.

30

The suction of my time above pulled my flapping coat as I lunged. I had to force myself through thickness I couldn't see. I pushed with all my strength. The gate banged shut behind me. I breathed my native air like a drug, eyes blurring.

Fantie was laughing, his face crowded by a lot of bristly hair he grew to hide his startling beauty and his eyes that phosphoresced like twilight seas. "Has it been eternity already?"

"Of a sort," Sull said.

"Where're my rooks?"

*

We may have come from two different corners of our hyper-natural world, but Sull and I'd become twins through and through. For a century we had not been apart, not even after our fondest, grandest arguments, fights that set the birds to wing.

Now I could not find him.

We were free to be home for now. The Thunder-lord had gone to sleep and was not accepting new appointments for 300 years. Time enough to construct our strategy for the world above before being thrown into exile once again. As nature spirits, we could weave a lot of new threads in that time for earth-above. One of Sull's top agendas: Be especially kind to ravens.

To describe my homeworld means sensory overload and might require using out of place or even cliché utterances like glitter-frost and mushroom-bed and rainbow-bridge and houses made out of boots. But I will say the haunted forests to the north, and the bright-petaled lands to the south all spread under a sun of faceted topaz 300 times the size of planet Earth.

Fantie lived in a boot with windows and trellises and sill-boxes filled with flowers depicting the different phases of the moon. I went there to ask after Sull.

"He had some mission. Didn't say when he'd be back. He didn't even finish the game." He indicated his marble and diamond-encrusted chess board. It was covered with miniature, partial castles. There were no other pieces, just the rooks.

"He didn't say where? Or what direction?"

Fantie scratched his autumn-nut brown hair. Shook his head.

"What did you guys talk about all these weeks?"

"Oh wine, of course. And acorns and Mozart. Tao te ching. Knitting. The usual."

I had gone south to visit my brothers who, as always, were all too busy to talk. I walked a disappointed journey. I missed Sull.

"Maybe he didn't say where he was going," Fantie said. "But…" He looked at the ground beyond his boot-heel patio, gesturing to the soft, tan dirt. In the dust were marks shaped like little triangles. "He makes pointy prints wherever he goes."

I grinned at him. "Thanks."

*

Sull sat in a peach grove where night had flung an arm. He wore his striped socks, knickers forged of silk and gold, a poet's shirt with undone ribbon cuffs. One hand moved darkly, covered in his black-lace glove.

In the other hand he held something I could not see. The black-lace fist moved up and down through the air. A lantern glowed by his thigh. He was sewing.

Behind him a wooden ladder leaned against a tree trunk. In the branches of flashing leaves the ladder's end disappeared. I could not tell how high it went.

I watched him for awhile, his fugitive focus, his pure resolve.

"I know you're there," he finally said.

I stepped forward. "What's the ladder for?" Were we going to start smuggling peaches?

"Sooth." He kept sewing. I still couldn't see what. "One needs a ladder to touch the sky."

"One needs wings," I said, tasting bitter. "Or a rocket."

"Since we have neither…" He didn't finish.

"Why were you touching the sky?"

"I didn't. I wasn't tall enough."

He'd always wanted to be bigger. Was it all about that again?

"There. Finished." Something glimmered on his naked palm.

"What is it?" I came closer.

He held it on a gossamer thread. Like an ornament, it turned on its frame of twigs and within the weaves and tiny knots that held it all together I saw cattails and pearls, moonlight and broken glass. The more I looked, the more I saw. A cricket. Ice. Something blue. A needle. A handmade velvet heart. Thorns. The wine-skin sky.

Sull said, "I know. I know. It's ugly." He reached up as far as he could and tied it to a button at my chest. "You lost your talisman. And that stupid plastic pony. I couldn't stop thinking about it. I couldn't reach the stars so I made you one. It's a great failure. I had hoped to do better. But at least it can be a shadow of what's real for now."

An ache inside my throat took my breath. Sull went dim and hazy.

He stared at me with tilted head. "No need for words." Then he held out his web-gloved hand. "Come on. The peaches are ripening. And we only have 300 years."

Thin as Rain

the days are made of silk
steam
and stars
nights are portents
auroras
immortal
ghosts come down from
the million skies of time
thin as rain and blue-backed
gusting into my mind
they bring candle-thoughts
lightspeed
the scent of alien fall

The Sibyl's Kitchen

The steam, like a hazy day, rose from the pot on the silver stove. Scent of burnt sugar. Scorched rain.

Dust on the wood plank floor. Gold sparkles. Underneath that, blackness. Thick and endless like time. Like the maze of a never-ending cave.

The sibyl's kitchen stood apart, alone, suspended in a thundercloud, in uncut tresses of shade.

The windows looked like carved squares of black marble. Unreal. But in truth they opened to views of stillness and cold and trapped time-death that swirled in a constant grief-shed blackness. Delicate but yellowed lace curtains did nothing to soften the view.

Candlelight and the flame under the strange stove gave off the only light. Nectarine. Opulent. Amber ashy glare.

The room and nothing else remained. Its walls, its windows and its contents were all.

Every night when Lissa dreamed, this was where she came.

Sometimes a woman sat at an old table as the contents on the stove boiled unchecked. Whatever was boiling let sparks of quicksilver snap into the air. Sometimes the sparks vanished instantly. Other times they floated around the room making constellations of unknown myths.

The woman sat before a globe. She had long braid-knotted hair, dark and wild as any jungle, and yellow-green eyes like cats-eye marbles. She was not old and not young. She wore scarves the color of multiple dusks, muggy blues and thin greens, and the pinks of past girlhoods. The scarves wrapped her whole body, dangling at her legs. Her rings prickled from her fingers like trapped lights, old fireflies blinking off and on.

The kitchen was summer and gold trapped in endless night.

The sibyl's globe held tiny planets, little Earths, as if a hundred spaceships had captured a hundred varied views from as many different times.

Lissa watched the globe and tried to figure it out but nothing about it made any sense.

When the sibyl was present, she acknowledged Lissa. She called Lissa 'Hope.' Lissa would sit and watch the globe until the dream ran out.

Sometimes Lissa dreamed the kitchen when the sibyl wasn't there. In the dust under the sill of one black window lay a naked man sleeping. He, too, was not always there. When he was there, he lay chained and unconscious. The chains extended from one wall, links thick as her arm, pitch against the shining flax of him where they wrapped his wrists and ankles, draping the chiseled valley of his waist. He was sun-chromed, though there was no sun.

Autumn-long hair winged against his eyelids. Every time she would go to him and touch his face, push back the silky hair. He never moved. He breathed slowly. Indifferent. His sleep was still.

In dreamtime she examined him, youthful enough, handsome but flawed. His scars at first terrified her. Shocked her. More than once she woke weeping at the memory of the white lines on his thighs, the shaft of his maleness, also scar-striped, dangling against an empty, puckered sac. Someone had made him a eunuch. Cruelly.

Every night she had the same dream or a variation of it. The kitchen. The indigo sibyl. The gelded man.

*

She gasped awake.

Lying beside her on frayed silks and broken cushions set against the stone, Lucius said, "Devil-girl."

Her twin brother hated her. Blamed her. For everything.

36

Their world lay on the cusp of constant storm. Threat. Demon-huddled skies overhead, ruins in the sands at their feet. War. Disease. Famine. Only the rich had survived. And only some of them.

She'd been lucky to be born a princess. But unlucky, too. For what life was to be had if you could not leave your home for fear of the black ash blizzards that came without warning, marauders who might carve the meat right off your bones while you yet still lived?

It had not always been so. Tales told of a once thriving world of mechanized convenience and pleasantry. Abundant food. Sunshine. Seasons. Cities and schools and farms. Offices, televisions, cell phones. Oceans, forests. Rain and snow. No ash. No soot. No char-faced lands.

She did not remember those times although she had been born into them. She'd been five, almost six when everything changed.

In Lissa's life she'd known few people. Seven families lived by the grottoes deep in the caves where fresh water still burbled. They'd fought and bought their way to this survival, their great wealth translating to hoarded food and other supplies while the poor had starved years ago. They'd traded smartly, diamonds and gold for guns and knives and caches of canned foods back when diamonds and gold still meant something.

That had been thirteen years ago.

Lucius turned on the wrinkled, makeshift bed, a bed fit for a princess only in this black world, and grabbed her shoulders. "I hate you." His eyes forced her gaze, black and predatory, hurt and mad. "Everything about you."

He pushed at her old torn gown; she felt it fall like a whisper from her shoulders.

She shoved his hands away.

He came back at her. Black hair, black eyes. Lips coarse as coal, hot, falling against hers.

He held her down. She squirmed, yelled into his mouth, pulled up with her knees to try to knock his body off her. He rolled more into her, his weight greater, his will, his strength.

Everything he did was his right. He was under orders. But she did not like to make it easy.

"I hate doing this," he said. "I hate it. I hate it!"

Lucius was one of only two fertile males left in all the seven families who was old enough to breed. The other fertile males were still babies, or still under ten years old. The elders had gotten it in their heads that babies were the future. Lissa only saw children as more mouths to feed in an already dead world.

The only other male of age, Darius, had fallen and hit his head two months back. The injury had blinded him and left him a drooling fool. All the of-age girls still not pregnant now relied on Lucius. Being his sister did not exempt Lissa's duty, nor Lucius'.

He hated her because she forced him to rape her. She hated him because he did rape her.

To think they'd once shared a womb seemed impossible now. Their wrath unborn would've torn their mother asunder.

He hit her. She hit back.

Once a week he had her and still she failed to quicken. He always took her in the morning when he woke naturally stiff, for she knew her presence and attitude did nothing to aid the burn in his veins.

As she kicked, he prodded her, staring at her body in the rags of silk. "You're ugly," he whispered.

She hissed, "Not as hideous as you!" In truth, he was strong and dark, and gleamed in the dim green light on the grotto walls. His hips were lean and smooth, his breath like fire.

His muscles and his force beat her in all ways and her legs fell open. She was not aroused, though, and so he hurt her. She scratched her nails across his back. He thrust and called her a cunt. The pressure inside her infuriated her. When he closed his eyes she knew he went somewhere else. He told her anywhere, even fucking the Devil in Hell, was better than being here with her underneath him. But he'd been given an order and he took to orders like a soldier. Going against the wishes of the community of families didn't occur to him. He didn't think about options, not even when they'd played as children. Lissa had always been the imaginative, hopeful one. He'd always been the obedient one. He knew he was right to do as he was told but somewhere deep inside him he also knew he was wrong. The resulting anger always blamed her.

Squinted shut, eyes lines of stressed, dark fringe, he looked suddenly so pained, so miserable that her body reacted in a wash of sadness, trembling. She was suddenly very sorry.

His eyes opened. Water filled them quavering on the brims of his lower lids. She breathed in sudden empathy. He saw it, quick as a flash, the pity within her, and his brow wrinkled as he gave her more quick thrusts. Her skin quivered. He said in a voice soft but dangerous, "If you come I'll kill you."

His lips pressed tight. She felt him let go. His eyes closed. The moisture from them scattered across her face.

He pulled away fast and was on his feet, leaving. She barely had time to find a loose stone, curl her fingers around it and throw it as hard as she could at his back. It hit him but he did not stop. He did not look back.

*

They ate rough porridge in china bowls with sterling silver spoons. The spoons had tarnished to a jaundice tint. The long, antique oak table separated Lucius and Lissa so they didn't have to look at each other.

She wore a necklace of diamonds to breakfast today, worthless as sand. Lucius always wore his gold Rolex on his left wrist. It still worked. Its value? Dust.

Fifteen other adults, children and babies sat around the table in hushed conversation. The cadence of the fresh underground spring rushed the air, the happy splash of water falling into a large, clear, open pool. Should that sound ever stop, they'd all be dead.

The porridge smelled of grime and earth and grotto water. It was cold. No one complained.

When she finished eating, Lissa wandered off to the deeper depths of the cave where no one would bother her, taking only one homemade candle. The glowworms on the walls and ceilings gave enough, dim, greenish light that she would not become lost. She usually had her share of chores to see to, but on the days Lucius had been assigned to her no one admonished her. No one ordered her around. They let her be.

The irony was if she got pregnant, Lucius' visits would stop. The families would all celebrate. And she would have no days off until she was ready to give birth. But more than she hated Lucius, she hated the idea of bringing a child into this corpse of a world. She did not want to get pregnant. Nor did she feel any compulsion to further the human species past this current generation. In all of it, she saw no point, no solution, only a useless game of eating, breathing and contemplating the shadows that trapped them all.

They were forbidden to leave the caves, but Lissa often thought about it. Going outside. Finding her own death in her own private way. Strangely, she felt left behind by death. Everyone else had gone. Where? She couldn't know. She felt wayward, not lucky. A princess under a curse.

To the stone walls she asked, "Who will come to kiss me and wake me from this spell?" Her voice echoed the only answer.

Water trickled from the moist rock with a bright green luminescence. It was harmless. She licked the sweetness, tongue going round and round the rock.

Later, she sat in a cozy alcove with her candle unlit between her legs. The muggy air surrounded her. The stone was cool. She slumped and slept.

*

A dusk-furred spider, penny-sized, zagged across the wooden table vanishing underneath. Twin moons rose and set in the silver steam from the boiling kettle on the stove. The air stung tart in her nose, acrid, sweet.

Breath fluttered the dusty air from the golden man in chains by the window, still sleeping.

"Stir the pot," a voice said.

Lissa could not see the sibyl but she felt her near, a shadow brush, a dark cold at her back.

Lissa stood by the stove, looking down, wooden spoon poised. The starry broth whirled, hummed, popped. The black soup bent back on itself as if in pain. Glitter made it shine. Wooden spoon and chaos, a rambling brew. Every round the spoon made pitched new patterns, endless. It was a constellation of everything jumbled in one place.

The voice of the sibyl, deep with age but soot-smooth, said, "Three things. He cannot be unbroken. Endings never end. Do not look back."

The stew was a mess. Lissa wanted to cry. In her mind she saw the sun itself was sad. On her ghost-world, it hitched and set in all the wrong directions. No clocks could be set by it because it might not rise again for days, if ever.

Here the windows shone only black. There was no worry about suns or time. Everything seemed contained and safe: the universe spitting in the cauldron, the tiny, hundreds of Earths preserved in a scrying globe, the only man in the room safely chained. He could not get at her.

It was safe, all safe, better than black howling winds and unknown futures. Better than living in cave-dark the rest of her life and waking up to her brother's duty.

Finally Lissa answered the sibyl.

"Then can I stay?"

*

He thought of all the stories of all the worlds he had ever known and saw them breaking, scattering, pieces of the lives of trillions of someones turned to falling stars, to rain.

The dungeon where he'd received his torment still remained within him. He breathed blood and fetid leavings and ancient sweats of pain.

The prince had chained him there, given torture orders with no questions.

The night of his downfall whispering ghosts cavorting with rumors tried to comfort him. All they did was remind him he could not die.

But he could be unmanned and thieved of his throne, his godhood. A sleek throne made of folded space from where he reigned over all of Time.

The rumors in his blackened hell foretold, in phantom hushes, of a sacred jar unlocked and all the evils within released.

All of Time lived within him, and because of that opened jar, every daemon, every destroyer, too.

Time and all its plays broke with a bit of help from the prince who came, possessed, and took it all. The prince of broken time, this new mad god-king was also his son.

He woke in a field of pre-dawn umber, meddling ash, all the burnt seasons settling around him. Winter-soot. Spring-cloud. Summer-smoke. Autumn-pitch.

He was still bleeding, helpless in locked chains, when the sibyl found him.

"The years flounder," he cried. "I forget their order or how they look. All the worlds suffer now. Time dreams me but I don't know where I am."

The sibyl said, "It is a puzzle," and picked him up in her night arms, chains and all, and brought him to her room.

For years he scryed his mind for the births of suns and seasons, but got only devil's eyes. More blood. Time was barren and so could not be sensed or reasoned with. His son ruled only a broken forever now, had no power to heal or even re-start Time. He wondered if the prince had even tried to right things, or ever cared to.

Nothing could heal him but the sibyl made a broth to calm him. She put everything she could think of into it. She called it Possibility Soup.

It took forever to cook.

When it was done she promised to feed it to him.

He waited and slept the void away. He dreamed of the empty evil jar. Hephaestus-forged. Pandora-owned. The banes and calamities unleashed upon the Earth.

Who would order such a thing to exist? Ah, the tricks of dreams spun back upon themselves to become dreams within dreams. The story turning lucid but the wrong way. Stories of all possibilities.

He dreamed the jar and stirred his hands in the leftover dusks, then lifted the lid to look underneath, see what might be left behind.

Sunset or sunrise—who could tell? But a little light blinked in all the storms. A faerie light barely beaming, like a piece of glitter stuck fast.

It might be coaxed.

Willed not to wither.

That was the first time the cursed princess came and touched his hair.

*

Lissa woke in the depths of the dim cave. Angry. To stay asleep forever. That had been her wish.

She got up, dusting off her silken rags, forgetting the candle. With silent steps she made her way down a narrow side passage. Eventually it led to a steep incline and sandier ground.

Not the main entrance, but another one. Blocked. Set with booby traps.

She knew each trip wire, every string.

Avoiding them, she crawled through a passage she and another child had dug years—or maybe eons—ago, to peek at the outside world they were forbidden to enter. To see for themselves the overcooked, blackened land. Seeing was believing. They'd needed to know.

Only adults had ever gone out there. And only twice that she knew of.

In impenetrable night they'd seen nothing. As promised, lightless lands and dank unknowns lay beyond. Ash filled their mouths, stung their eyes. The smoke-sweet burn in her throat left a pinprick of pain that had never gone away. She felt it now. The little excursion had given her nightmares for months.

But she wasn't a scared kid anymore. She was a trapped woman in a black shell casing. Even if impossible, she wanted to break it, tear herself free.

She had very little thought when she emerged from the tunnel and felt the cave walls give way to open air.

It was not quite how she remembered it, this outside, this ruined stage.

Black fog bled down from the sky. The scent was cinder char. What gravitated toward her like fear was the silence. So absolute.

She'd been five when the world ended. It hadn't happened all at once; it took awhile.

She remembered frightened adults hushed and talking in the great room of her childhood home. Then moving boxes and big, filled-to-the-brim trucks. Strange things her parents bought. Gadgets that worked with wound gears and no electricity. Tools. Long silver guns.

Other adults had met with her parents, arguing, weeping sometimes.

She remembered the desperate night they'd abandoned their large house with the two pools, the tennis courts, the corrals. She and Lucius had cried because they'd had to leave behind most of their toys and games. The long trip to the mountains had made her sick.

Once they situated themselves in the caves and were told they were "camping" by their parents, big trucks came and went, forever it seemed, unloading goods. Non-perishables, they called them. Everyone helped carry and cart these supplies to the deeper rock rooms.

Twice over thirteen years men went out into the endless nights, the coal-mists, and using hoarded gas brought more truckloads. They foraged dead warehouses slumped in forever shadow. Because of these trips, food, carefully doled, lasted for years. They could also fish in the green-lit grottoes with some success as well. But mostly when it wasn't fish somehow preserved in this underground water source, the food was paste, or canned, unrecognizable greens.

The food would run out some day even if it took a hundred years. But Lissa heard the adults talk and plan for farming once the black season passed. When would that be? Another ten years? Fifty? No one knew.

The adults had refused to give up and die. Probably she should have been grateful. But she wasn't because their plan included babies. The next generation. All were in agreement over expanding their numbers. But they found out too soon all but the very young were sterile.

The bookworm Lissa, the escapist, rebelled. Maybe this was all there was. The Earth had nothing left to give. Growing up knowing virtually nothing else except what she read in books, how could she hope for that new Earth which she'd never experienced? It'd be easier to write the tale than try to live it all over again.

Monsters out of the dark came to her in nightmares. This was no place to thrive.

She stood before the cave's side entrance, night hot and dry upon her brow. A distant wind keened as if the world cried. A death-echo.

Something darker than the ashen night flapped over her head and was gone. Something living?

She moved into the darkness unafraid.

*

The sibyl said to him, "Drink."

But he couldn't quite wake, couldn't quite see let alone open his mouth, or swallow.

Fingers combed his hair. A hand behind his head helped him lift. His eyelids quivered. There was light and that was all.

Something warm and smooth pressed his lips. A cup. No, a bowl. Fizzing liquid filled his mouth. Sweet burning drowned his throat. The taste was everything: sugared wind, star-ash, dirt-salt, green water. The taste was silver, pulse, vacuum, sonic, time. Music and mint. Lore and luck. Mother. Woe. Nuclear.

His eyes opened and he spun. Or the room did, golden and steamy, lacy and amorphous.

Heavy chains clashed. He heard a gong, felt a pain. Something struck the heavy links over and over and the vibration of it rattled his muscles, tugged painfully. He cried out, thrashed.

"Hold still!"

The sibyl struck again, heavy axe-head against tarnished captivity. She had put him here. Held him immobile. Now metal bent in hot strikes. And then, just like that, he was free.

He scrambled about until he sat. Then he stood shakily, and the dark-eyed woman before him met his gaze.

The sibyl's voice rasped. "You cannot go back."

"Such is the nature of time," he answered. Yet he wept.

Night captured me. Night set me free, he thought. For he knew her now, and remembered her names. Witch-of-evening. Midnight. Three A.M.

And his own names now also echoed in his mind. Hour. Year. Century. Chronos.

He wandered about the dusty, magical kitchen. The black windows and the sibyl silently watched.

He approached the table, sat, and for a long time stared into the globe of trapped Earths. When he was ready he made a fist. The shards of the globe flew about the room like a storm of glass snow. The Earths popped free and spiraled off, some vanishing right through the blackened windows into the nothing, some falling, clattering, some popping like bubbles in the air.

He got up and approached the flickering stove. For a long while he watched the blue-tipped flames dance and snap in its open recesses. He thought of his son and revenge. He thought of taking back his throne. Then he thought of the cursed princess who had occasionally visited, remembered her cool, smooth hand stroking his face. He stooped and stepped into the heat, one charred Earth decorated with a faint, flickering faerie light still clutched in his hand.

*

Lambent eyes like two meteors. Rumbling growl. Scent of musk and necropolis crypt-rot.

The sting of adrenaline ran just under the skin of Lissa's arms, back, neck. Knowing she was prey, Lissa still wondered that anything could still live in this cinder-world.

The shadow with the blazing eyes moved, huge and heavy, darker than the night as if it had wings that towered.

The breeze of it lifted her hair. Lissa knew each second now as a craved sweet. For here in the dark these would be her last thoughts. Of a once-blue world turned barrow. Of endless disinterment. Of monsters in the dark.

As she crouched there, tired, her feet burning, she could not suppress a whimper.

Suddenly the dark drew up. Something happened to the sky. A crack. A break. A wound. A flurry of gold fell from it like half-remembered leaves on pumpkin winds.

Blackness fractured.

With a low howl and a grunt, the black shadow breathing at her side loped away. She could see its bear-like shape vanish among lesser shadows. Everything grayed, dusky and twi-lit. Then she saw the broken, copper sun, twisted in the sky but still bright. Like hope.

Sight returned and she found herself standing in a silver glade of gray, stick-trees, a pond of mercury just beyond. Slowly everything brightened. The pond went tourmaline. The trees stood in topaz relief. Everywhere, tickling the ground, were little green shoots. Air misted fresh, unburnt against her damp face.

Further toward the hills came a green light. A blue horizon. The dark had kept her from seeing it. But now, as if someone had lifted the lid of a cursed jar, light and life seeped around her.

Endings never end, the sibyl had said. Darkness still framed the day, as if the world were suspended in endless black. But the glade whispered to itself in wordless secrets that took no heed of it.

Lissa moved deeper into the new season and did not look back.

Who Sleeps?

Who sleeps in the moon of my window?
Gusty rags of clouds
furl north to freeze
flocks of shadows
and my world
through the golden spyglass
of memory
I open my eyes in the blue stars
Who is sleeping there
in the shaded ruins of
all the time-poisoned voids?

Message From the Lantern

And even if you put me into a bottle
And throw me in the sea
I will come back
I will tell lies

*

I have a story to tell about an eternal alien, a ghost who cannot move on, and the desperate madnesses of time like scattered stars. It may seem liquid and convoluted. I am not sure that I can tell it any other way.

There is a cage. Well, there are many cages. Perhaps too many to count: The prisons of our thoughts. The locked-down limitations of a human body. Possessive love. Debt. Jail, or sexual control, or bolted rooms created for one's own safety. Belief systems are cages. Even a clock can be a cage.

But in my story, while avoiding these other implements of incarceration, I've lived encased for a very very long time in a six by six inch sealed lantern, a construct kept intact by my own ancient divination to withstand the tumbles and passions of the sea, a device of magic and salt condensation and the most exquisite isolation a being could ever know.

Centuries pass like flickers of a dream. Still, I cannot solve the puzzle that is me.

Caught in his own cage of belief or fear or perhaps simply true love, Jet tried to help.

In fact, it was Jet who locked me here and threw me into the sea. Jet who tried to kill me.

But if I were to start at the beginning, not my real beginnings but the moment I first acquired a memory, Jet was also the one who found me.

Should I start there? On the beach in Greece where I washed ashore like a pallid dead thing and took a startled first breath when strong, golden arms wrapped around me?

Or should I begin with the mystery that is myself?

For now, perhaps I will simply ramble. These are, after all, notes from a monster no one will ever read.

My cage is a quantum house. Technically, it cannot exist. Should not exist. But it does.

There are three rooms but I could make more. But three is enough for me now. Bedroom with connected washroom. Front room with couch, library, and in more recent times of technological advent, TV and computer. And a kitchen of sorts, although I never need to cook. Accessories appear and disappear as I wish. Making those items work, like the television when I have no reception, works for me in the same way that objects just come to me. It's all in a wish.

Except for the accessories appearing at my command, sounds fairly ordinary, I'm sure, but it's not. This magical place is contained within my tiny lantern prison. The lantern itself has three framed glass 'walls', the fourth being a solid iron one.

After everything, I really couldn't blame my lover for locking me in here and throwing me away. I am, we surmised, a Marid, a jinn, and my very existence can always bring harm to those who cross my path. I have never met another like me. And if you find me and release me from my eternal prison I will be the elixir who gives you a wish.

As I write this very paragraph, Jet pops in for a visit. Being a ghost, he can do that now. It wasn't always like that. For so long I was alone after he threw me into the sea. In death, for him time moves differently. It seemed like it took him hundreds of years to find me in order to haunt me. We're bound together, me and him.

"Trin," he says, for despite being long dead, and my betrayer, he visits me often, alternately torturing and comforting me in a love/hate relationship that requires no forgiveness. "Hurry, the game's on."

He's sitting incandescently on my couch, waiting for me to pop in refreshments.

Bored, I wave my hand. Two beers and a bowl of chips appear on the coffee table. Of course ghosts can't eat or drink, but this is magical sustenance. He can chomp down on magic chips to his heart's content and sometimes I think that's his main reason for sticking around.

The house rocks. My silks and satins (for I crave luxury) cover the blackness behind the glass walls but the incessant motion of my home always reminds me I am living beneath the torments of a thousand tides, lost to the dark-finned depths.

And all thanks to Jet over there who picks up his beer, guzzles a moment, then burps.

We may appear to be two "regular" guys but we are not. And just because I have been in my male form for a thousand years and some, do not assume anything about me.

I was female once and may well be again. But attachment to form is one of my weaknesses. And I really enjoy this one, tall, mocha-hued, black hair to my waist. When I was female this was my "type." Although we can touch, my ghost lover is of very little use to me anymore since his ghost body does not experience feeling as intensely as his human one did and so his "appetite" is off. Since I often have only myself to keep me company, I keep this form.

Jet is entertaining, though, and more company than I'd have had he not been compelled to come from death to search for me and pledge, in the name of love, to remain in eternal internment with me. His pledge is subject to whim, however, since he can pop in and out of my lantern at will and once left me alone for fifty long years of perpetual salt condensation and me thinking he'd stopped loving me and trying to forget him.

Endless seas and endless time. These are my comas.

"Trin, what ARE you doing?" Jet mutters from the velvet-tasseled couch.

"Trying to figure things out," I say, typing. The computer screen is filled now with my little dark-lettered thoughts.

"What, you mean like taxes?" He laughs at his own joke.

"Uh-huh."

The house rolls gently. The little lamp lifting on a deep tide.

I don't know where I come from. I have no memory of being a child, or of parents. It is all a blank. Am I a created being? Unnatural? Or some sort of spontaneous manifestation? Am I someone's long-lived spell? Am I even real?

Questions I've asked myself for centuries on end. I can't answer.

Jet is a blond, rare among his kind back in the day, with hematite eyes always searching. While alive, he was a philosopher and a scientist, a boundless swirl of energy almost never at rest, and always getting into trouble with "the tribe." He questioned everything, beliefs, ritual, custom. He scared people. They didn't like to hear what he might spout. But since he is intrinsically incapable of shutting up, he pissed off many of the wrong sort. After he found me on that wild beach in Greece and nursed me back to health, I became a sort of guard for him. I was in female form when he found me. But when he found out I could change form at will, I had a use. I could be big and intimidating. This ability of mine enchanted him. He couldn't stop touching me, even in my different forms. I found I didn't mind.

He's one of the most intelligent people I've ever known, almost annoyingly so, but he did spend much of his life trying to solve the puzzle of me. Though he tried to destroy me, I am indebted to him.

Right now he's talking again, mostly to himself, the hooting of the game on in the background. "...people getting paid to study about universes colliding..." "...the one with the dog and the boat and the cell phone..." "...Tarzan, yeah, the all-time best character...or Sherlock Holmes maybe...or Achilles...I can't decide..." "...all that infernal buzz, twenty-four/seven; can't tell time by the TV anymore..."

After Jet found me and I slowly came to understand where I was, that I was alive, and that despite amnesia I could speak his language, we together discovered my abilities that clued us in that I was not human. The first time I remember anything odd was when I was lying in his bed, dozing and dreaming in a kind of fever from my uncounted time at sea. I felt thirsty. I called for him. No response. I stared at the white plaster wall in front of me, listened to the sea rasping outside, the sounds of the sea-birds, the wind's endless quest. My dry mouth tried to swallow. I needed water. Now. I lifted the light cover, raised my hand and a ceramic cup appeared in the air before me. At first I thought Jet had snuck in behind me and I just didn't see him. But there was nothing holding the cup but air. I reached out, took it, drank from it. Pure, sweet water. Perfect.

At that moment, Jet came in with a cup. Gently, he said, "You're awake. I thought you might be thirsty."

I held out the cup.

"Where'd you get that?"

I shrugged.

"That's not one of mine."

"It just appeared," I said.

He thought I'd gotten up, gone out. But I had not. Despite the beauty of my then female form, and his immediate attraction and dedication to me, he did not believe me. So I showed him. I wished for the cup to vanish. It did.

For a whole minute he was speechless. My body was shaking. I feared...I don't know what. Maybe that he'd throw me away, hurt me. I did not know then that I could not die.

54

My vision tremored as I watched his dark eyes. Then his voice came. A whisper. Relief like an answered prayer. "Do it again."

I decided to be more imaginative. This time I hoped for a small table of food. Behind him, it appeared. As he stared at it in obvious shock, he said sensibly, "The people cannot know how dangerous you are."

"I'm bound to you," I said, like one of his many hapless, moony paramours. "I do only as you wish." Why I said that, I do not know. But to this day, I know it's true, in my heart, my bones. He found me. And I am his.

"I have no wishes except for you to stay."

After that, the women stopped coming to his rooms and making noise in the night. I became his sole focus, although he hid me away for a long time.

I enjoyed the comfort of him, the care. He took charge of everything. Abandoned by my memory, often confused, I let him. I became whatever he wanted when he wanted it. When he finally trusted me enough to let me outside into the world, admonishing me to never use my gifts in public, I appeared in male form, his bodyguard, for his views of the world did not mirror those of common times, and he often got into fights. He had three different teaching jobs and was fired from all three. The research studies he excelled at got him into trouble when he spoke or wrote on the various subjects, political, theological, even magical.

But the best part was he studied me as well, reading any ancient scripts he could find that might describe me. One day he found the word "Marid" which meant a type of jinn, a sea-jinn or genie.

"Where do they come from? Who are they?"

"It gives no origin. Just that they once existed like angels or the Sidhe."

"But where do I come from? Who are my people?"

He just shook his head. None were known in our time one thousand years ago, or now. And I never met any. What worried him was the myth about granting wishes. We discussed it. At the time I had no compulsion to grant wishes in the manner of the old fables, although I gave myself whatever I needed, and I never turned down any request of Jet's. With him it was all about my will, my love.

But Jet was a philosopher. He ranted about people and their inherent laziness, their ways of stupidity and perversion. He saw a world of sheep and the occasional farmer, of a hive with the occasional queen. He believed in the wrong hands I would be enslaved and tortured to provide things, large things, that would not be good for the world. He said, "If anyone were to get hold of you, force you... Human wishes are almost always seeded with a hidden violence."

He believed if we did not keep my secret that I might suffer terribly. And that the world would most certainly be destroyed.

"Trin, what are you writing at so diligently over there? Do you have an Internet lover again? Are you one of those boring sorts on Facebook?" His voice interrupts my memory, that soft, low accent he has when he speaks English. I turn to look at him, half in the past, half in my enchanted lantern gazing at this handsome, ancient ghost.

"I'm writing a story."

He frowns. "What story?"

"My story."

"Who will you ever show it to?"

"Well, you for one."

"I already know your story."

He wants attention. That's all. I can't resist him. But before I quit and join him on the velvet couch I want to put down on the computer the events of that day centuries ago. The day Jet tried to kill me.

*

56

We had been together, happily, for five years. I had done my duty to him in that I had obeyed his command to never reveal my true self to any other living soul. We had made contingency plans, too, should anything ever go wrong.

Jet was smart. He thought ahead. He was also very protective. He and I discovered together that I had the ability not only to change my appearance, but I could make myself very very small. This meant that I could easily hide should anyone ever threaten me. Still, we had no idea that I was not simply a long-lived creature, that I could not die. We did not know that I could reanimate myself from any disaster that might befall me. Why would we assume such a thing? There were no others of my kind anywhere that we could find. We figured they'd all become extinct, wiped out by a far distant, violent past.

Because I could make myself so small, he and I realized there were almost an infinite number of objects I could hide in, for days and weeks if I needed to, because I could manifest food and necessities at will. I could easily fit in shells, bottles, locked boxes. I could be stored away in perfume phials, toy drawers, overturned cups on saucers. I could roll around in hollow egg shells, sleep in a log, wile away the hours in covered buckets. The problem was I found that once I was inside one of these containers I felt stuck. I could create comforts for myself, but I could not leave. I would wish hard, think myself outside and big, but nothing would happen. Only when Jet would command, "Come, Trin. Come to me," could I release myself, as if all the air in my lungs finally was allowed to escape and I could breathe again. Be again.

We realized that without an outside voice to focus on, (any command would do,) I could not return to the larger world. I could not move.

The magic astounded us. And frightened us. Jet was afraid I'd become stuck if anything happened to him, so he commanded me to never hide unless I felt I was in extreme life-threatening danger.

The day came when that happened. Jet had gone on a day trip to visit friends. I had not wanted to accompany him and demanded to be left home. I hated most of his friends anyway, and I really was not the social type. Wives back then were more homebodies anyway, even the childless ones, and men who dragged their wives to scholarly social gatherings were rare. Even if I'd chosen to go with him in male form, I still would've been ostracized. And bored. His friends could sense something different about me. When I was around them, I was often challenged. I hated other people.

So I stayed home and played at redecorating for the thousandth time, wishing the walls from purple to red to yellow, changing the furniture around from settees to low beds to throne-back chairs, amusing myself with all the ways I could set up house in Jet's seaside, whitewashed abode. Also, I knew it irritated him when I changed things up, so I did it often.

While I was at my game, losing myself in color and swirl and the ultimate magic of my power, I did not notice until too late a small face peering through a front window, the neighbor boy, Poa, who was not yet six years old.

Usually I was extremely careful, covering all windows and doors before doing anything so blatantly magical. Today I had curtained everything but one small window. A forgotten window on the leeward side facing the ocean and a cliff. No one ever went by there. The wall was narrow and there was no walkway. Below was only the crashing sea.

But a brave, climbing boy of five could balance there on a dare. A boy of five might scramble like a monkey on that wall and never fear of falling.

When I noticed him it was too late. He'd seen everything. All my tasks. My talents.

I could not think what to do. I didn't want to confront the boy. I had no idea what I might say to him. I did not deal well with children. But I worried that he'd run off, tell his parents or other children. Our secret would be out, then. Mine and Jet's.

Frozen in mid-spell, I locked my gaze with his. Suddenly, he scrambled away from the wall and I heard his sandaled footsteps running up the stairs to my door. "Trin! Mrs. Trin!"

I heard him at the door and before I could think I had popped myself into a nearby vase. The boy would find the house empty, I hoped, and think perhaps he had dreamed it all.

Poa's mother let him run wild. The boy had no manners at all. But he'd never come into our house without invitation. Never. Until now. He opened the door when he did not hear my response. "Trin!" he called. "You make magic. I see! I wanna see!"

Finding an empty house, I could hear him wander from room to room, calling my name. I did not respond. I couldn't until commanded. I would have to wait for Jet to come home before I could call to him in my tiny voice and beg him to command me to come out. But then the little boy, perhaps wise beyond his years, said, "Trin, I know you hide. Come out, Trin. Come to me." And the overwhelming surge I felt every time Jet commanded me pushed through me like a harsh, warm wind. The breath I needed to take came up. The release exploded within, and I suddenly found myself standing before Poa. I had panicked as I felt that surge, and taken my larger, male form. I towered over him.

He gaped, his mouth wide open, his dark eyes big as coins. He took a faltering step back on his short, stubby legs. "You not Trin."

"I am." The strange compulsion to be honest with him overwhelmed me. I felt utterly at this boy's mercy, as if I now belonged entirely to him.

"But you're a boy!"

"Sometimes," I replied, again far too honest than I had planned. This was not going well at all, and as if I were a puppet on a string, I had no control. Jet and I had never foreseen any such event as this, that I would be bound to anyone who might find and release me from any sort of self-imposed hiding place or prison. The fact that that person might be a child, naïve and thoughtless, was terrifying me now.

Against my will, I heard myself speak, as if compelled, controlled by some unseen force. "Poa, I am Trin. You have released me. What are you doing here, child? What do you wish?"

He put his hands behind his back and rocked side to side, pouting. "I ran away."

"You didn't get far. You live only next door."

"I only just started," he replied, blinking at me as if he still couldn't believe I was who I said I was. "Trin is a girl," he said, finally, as if trying to make sense of things.

"Sometimes." Again, I found I could only tell the truth. I couldn't move from his gaze. I wanted Jet to come home. I wanted to run and find him, have him smooth things out himself with the boy, but I could not budge.

Finally, some recognition lightened his eyes. "I know you. You come around sometimes for Jet. When people want to fight him. You guard him."

"Yes."

Then abruptly, he said, "I hate my parents. I ran away. I wish they were dead! I wish you could guard me!"

*

I sit typing this, listening to Jet shift around impatiently on my couch.

If I had one day to do over… If Jet had only come home half an hour before he did.

Wishes, once done, cannot be undone. That is my fate, and the fate of those who cross my path.

60

*

The earthquake happened in the afternoon, just as Jet walked through the door to our home. It devastated the village. Many people were injured. Two died. The two were Poa's mother and father. The only house left fairly unharmed was mine and Jet's.

Jet, it turned out, had been coming up the steps when he heard the boy make plain his wish. He knew what I had done.

"Trin!" The world shifted. We all stumbled, scrambling for balance, as outside the screams started and the destruction began.

For about two minutes it seemed the world had come to an end. The boy screamed and ran outside in fear.

Afterwards, Jet came toward me, crazy-eyed. "What have you done?" He grabbed me. I was bigger, stronger, but I never raised a hand to him. "Are his parents dead?"

I nodded, my throat too swollen with regret to speak.

His hands went around my neck. "Trin! It's wrong! It's wrong. Those were people!"

The fingers squeezed. In fear, I vanished from his grip to the nearest abode. An oil lamp framed in iron with three glass sides. I hid inside as Jet turned around and around, yelling for me. "Where'd you go?" He was furious. Panicked. Finally he saw movement in the lamp. He clamped the lid down, locked it.

For a long time nothing happened. I didn't see anything outside the glass. No movement. Then I realized he was holding me, sitting on the floor with his knees bent. And he was crying.

After about an hour, while there were still screams and disturbances outside, Jet moved through the open doorway and to the wall that had most recently been scaled by Poa. For a long time he stood, holding the lantern up, staring at the sea. Then suddenly I felt it. No sound, no word, just a feeling. He

61

had tossed me as far as he could and I felt myself falling, falling.

The crashing waves rose over me then. And that ended my life on land.

Later, when his ghost came to me, he told me he had searched for me, hoping I'd be washed ashore again. He'd regretted his impulsive decision. He loved me. He couldn't live without me.

But that night there had been a wild storm, wreaking even more havoc on the village, and the waves had carried me far, far out. Instead of pushing me ashore, as they might have on a calmer day, they took me in the lantern to depths I had no hope of rising from.

I thought I would never see Jet again.

For years I railed and cried against my glass, lantern prison. I babbled. I talked to myself. I tried to kill myself by not eating. Nothing happened. I manifested all kinds of weapons and stabbed, cut, impaled myself. I never died.

Later, years later, I created this home. When technology came to the world, I wished for all the luxuries of that and caught up on history and culture. I lost hundreds of years in a delirium. When Jet's ghost found me, the reunion was passionate and accusing. We came together in a wild frenzy of astonishment and awe, then didn't speak to each other for a week.

He was dead. A ghost. I was immortal. And trapped. Still tied to me, he couldn't move on. I couldn't be free. We blamed each other.

Magic bound us. He was my master forever.

*

"Trin! Come to me."

Already I feel the compulsion. My hands slow at typing this message. Already I can feel his presence beside me, his hands in my hair, the ghostly tingle of his touch.

I have no more time to type now. I'm sending this into world. To all my online friends, my entire address book. If you get this and you have any mercy at all, you will free me. All you need to do is write me back. Together we can end or begin the world. All you need to say in any returned message to me, if you dare, are these words:

"Trin, come to me."

I will be there.

I will be yours.

Jet can move on and I will be free.

Decree

inhuman now
her hair of greenest gold
rivers down night
from the highest black window
this violence
done to princesses
these icy spells
from the drowned diaries of
mermaid witches
must stop
these attic lock-downs
these cinder waifs
so decrees
the queen of Storyland

The Dream in a Box

The thing in the other room has just finished its breakfast of fried eggs and beets. It bellows for me to come clean up after it.

I go into the bedroom, smell the stink of sweat on sheets I haven't changed for three days. It begs for more pills.

"Not until eleven," I say.

It moans that it hates me. "Oh I hurt. I hurt." Its lips are stained purple from the beets. It looks like a cruel clown, an old child.

I turn on the TV news. It groans, says over and over, "Fuck you. Fuck you."

I ignore it as well as I can. Some days are easier than others to endure. Some days the thing can blubber and yell, spit and fart, and I am unmoved. Other days the scent, the suffering, the words of the thing are shards, and cut me deep, and the house becomes a jail, and I am imprisoned for something I haven't done.

I am innocent of all charges.

"I am innocent of all charges," I say aloud.

"Fuck you and get me my pills," it says. "It hurts!"

I turn, my composure exceedingly patient for a Saturday, and go into the hall. There I find clean sheets folded by my own hands, fluffed with softener, and I think, *You don't have it so bad,* "you" referring to the thing.

I go back into the bedroom. The thing is moaning, its reddish-stained mouth parting to reveal yellow teeth, a dark blot of tongue. It coughs and spits at me.

"Now I'm going to change the sheets," I say.

"Be gentle. Be gentle." It starts to cry.

I roll my eyes. Pull down the covers.

The thing has one arm and no legs. It is naked. It has red smears on its side, rose-shaped. These are its blister scars from when it was very sick. I rub oil into them every night. The hollow sockets of its hips dip into scars where legs used to be. I oil those as well. From the lump of its torso, genitals, withered and red, dangle. Sometimes, with its good hand, it strokes them, not even caring if I'm in the room.

The thing's hair is silver and long because I haven't cut it in awhile. Though I try to comb it every day, it remains tangled.

I gently roll the thing onto its side, despite its loud protests, and pull the sheet free from the mattress. The news babbles in the background about smog, war, new viruses, the environment we can conquer and rebuild through intellect and preservation. Strange, new diseases appear every day. Nothing changes. Nothing will ever change.

I go to the other side of the bed, roll the thing onto the scarred lump of what is left of its bad arm. It wails. I pull the whole sheet loose, ball it up.

The thing falls to its back again, looking up with dark, cold eyes. "You have no soul," it says.

"Ah, but I do have clean sheets." I repeat the process, putting on the clean bottom sheet. As I do so, the thing urinates, soiling the sheet. The plastic beneath catches most of it.

"You're supposed to ask for the bottle," I say. "Now we'll have to go through this all over again."

It whimpers, but it's smiling.

When I finish cleaning the thing, the morning is only half-gone. I have an hour before it'll demand lunch. I leave the thing dozing in front of the TV and head for my room, where the closet waits with the secret I have hidden there.

I keep my secret in a cardboard box on the top shelf behind my old photo albums of Mom and Dad and me when I was happy. I push aside the albums and slide the box into my arms. Cradling the package, I go to the bed and place it on the bedspread beside me.

Many people break the law. It's not even considered abnormal anymore to exist above the law, or below. But I still have some respect, instilled by my parents, perhaps, for rules that make life more pleasant on the whole, and for the legal process, which attempts to protect those who, by no fault of their own, become victims.

Therefore, every time I lift the lid on the box, I experience a twinge of doubt, a hesitation of fear. I cannot help but feel unclean, perhaps a little insane, for that first moment when the contents of the box are revealed.

Soon, however, I relax, and know that no amount of guilt can cause me to resist this piece of illegal magic, this pure form of desire.

The contents of the box are difficult to describe. What exists within is a kind of mist rainbowed with an oily sheen. The mist is home to a dozen or more pulsing, amber lights. Like fireflies, they play along the circuits of the rainbow, never repeating the same pattern twice. The scent of Christmas fills the room.

This is The Dream, a little piece of electric magic, captured dark matter, invisible except when mixed with warped, inside-out gravity-light puffs of energy. It is a self-contained piece of another reality. The stuff of creation, so some say; what the universe was formed from when nothing became something. No one knows who actually discovered it or invented it, or where it originated. In fact, officially, it does not exist. The rumor is that The Dream was destroyed by the government. Even now that all traces of it have supposedly been "eradicated," The Dream is considered so dangerous that to possess it or anything like it could get you twenty years in prison. It is a legend. A dark street fairy tale. I came upon it by luck. I would never find another one in a thousand years. The seller I bought it from, an old school friend, denies any association with reality pirates or products. He'd come upon a cache of The Dream by accident and just wanted to get rid of it fast. The one I got was the last of his supply. I spent everything I had to buy it.

All forms of reality-altering drugs and devices are illegal. Anything that goes into the brain and changes it, and is not a simple prescription for pain or a cure for disease, is illegal.

But this is different. It isn't a drug. It isn't a brain-controlling device. This, which I call The Dream, is unlike any of that stuff, completely unique. You have complete control over it. You can relive memories. And no new reality it shows you actually exists unless you decide, finally, to remain there and leave all other realities behind. You decide where it can take you, what to create.

I place my hands in the box and The Dream rushes to meet my body warmth with the soft snapping sound of static electricity. The energy seems intelligent, almost alive. I might go so far as to call it a creature, except that I have never noticed any independent reaction from it, other than the patternless flashing of lights and an aurora-pulsing of the mist, which gives the impression that The Dream is animate. The Christmas scent is a reflection of my own mind. Every time I open the box, I'm reminded of the enchantment of childhood Decembers; evergreens surrounded by brightly colored packages, the aroma of sugar cookies.

The nature of The Dream is to absorb thoughts and moods, and create out of that whatever the person holding The Dream wills it to create. Will is important, the seller told me. Will is like "soul." You infuse your will with the stuff of The Dream and you can go anywhere you wish, experiencing anything you desire. It is more than even a lucid dream. You are there. With The Dream, I can have Christmas as often as I want, or birthdays, or travel trips, or adventure limited only by my rustic imagination.

The Dream coats my hand with soft tingles. It is weightless. A breeze. A cloud.

The scent changes from Christmas to rain. I grin as the mist flows over my palms and wrists. The amber lights make the purples and greens and yellows of the moving rainbows look hot, fluorescent. Now the scents of flame and smoke.

"Henrick!"

Startled, I almost drop the box. The Dream twists; the edges wither as an ochre hue edges the rainbows, the fog.

"Henrick! The pain! The pain! Pills! Now!"

The call of the thing in the other room causes The Dream to squirm even more. The inner program that touches my hands and absorbs my will gives off scents of shit and steam. I hate when this happens more than anything, for this is the purity of life, of goodness, and to see The Dream, *my* dream, tainted in any way, makes me sick to the very center of myself. I need to keep it away from the thing.

If I dared enter The Dream now, with the thing's distraction and interruption, I'd simply relive a cruel reality exactly, or near to exactly, as wretched as the one I find myself caught in now.

I cannot stand to see The Dream respond like this. The sooner I settle The Dream back in the box, the sooner its healing can begin. I can try it again later.

Carefully, my hands lower the gossamer form to the cardboard container. Now that I am not in contact with its energy, the revolting ochre sheen in the mist turns to pink, then angel white. I smell freshly baked sugar cookies.

"Henrick!"

I drop the lid onto the box. "I'm coming!"

Into the closet, behind the photos, sequestered in darkness where nothing can touch the magic until I'm ready, I hide The Dream.

"Henrick!" The voice is agonized.

*

The thing is having a particularly bad day. It screams when I medicate and moisturize its scars. It spits food at me. It blubbers and assaults me with pornographic words. I try to ignore it as best as I can. I tell myself the thing is not really angry with me, but is frustrated by pain and suffering, by the condition of its warped form that causes the evil within to erupt uncontrolled.

If the thing gets worse, I know I can always call the doctor to come in earlier than her regularly scheduled visit. Sometimes, though, I think the thing needs an exorcist instead of an M.D. The thought offers me some much-needed amusement.

"What are you grinning at? Are you laughing at me?" the thing demands. With its good arm, it swings at me.

I easily duck and shake my head.

"You're nothing! You'll amount to nothing. You're too stupid to do anything worthwhile! You should never have been born!"

I finish tying back its hank of gray hair with a twisty, and set the comb aside. I really should cut the mess, but when it was younger, the thing liked to wear its hair in the fashionable ponytail of its lost era. A strange nostalgia keeps me from cutting it.

I reach for the electric shaver. It spits at me. "You are ugly and no good. Who wants you? Not me!"

"Then who'll take care of you?" I ask calmly, wiping the spittle from my arm.

"Edith."

"Edith isn't here."

"You lie! You're an abomination. You keep her from me. You've raped her. You've killed her. I know. And I'll turn you in to the police, you fat, ugly ..." The rest is too horrible to repeat.

Sometimes my inner calm is truly tried by the thing's vehemence. I understand that pain and misunderstanding cause hatred. And the hatred is almost always misdirected.

But I am overly sensitive about my weight and my less-than-average looks. And I am overly sensitive about Edith.

I cannot shave it when I am shaking, so I set the razor back on the table and turn away.

"You get Edith in here now! I want Edith!"

"Edith isn't here." I keep my back to it.

"That's because you killed her. You killed her!" It repeats its allegation over and over. I can hear a cry in its voice. Desperation. Mourning.

It is right about one thing. Edith is dead. But I am not the one who killed her.

*

The Dream is blue-tinted in my hands, scented with salt. The lights flicker sluggishly along muddy rainbows. Without another second's hesitation, I bring my hands up and press The Dream to my wet face.

Immediately, I am in the thing's room. It is bellowing and cursing. It has stained the bed with its eliminations.

I breathe through my mouth, short, timed puffs. It grins at me, yellow teeth caked with the mucus of dried spit. "You are a murderer," it says.

"This time," I say, "you are right." I take the carving knife from behind my back and plunge it into its quivering throat. Blood squirts into my eyes. I pull the knife out and watch the stream of red fountain onto the thing's chest. Its body twitches. Its mouth works silently, as though it wants to, but cannot, scream. It seems to take a long time for the thing to die. When it finally stops moving, I set to work carving what's left of its body into little pieces. These I dispose of down the kitchen garbage disposal. The bones I burn in the fireplace.

When I am finished, I take a hot shower. As I come out of the shower stall, I wipe the misted mirrors and stare at myself. In the mirrors, I am tall and broad-shouldered,

70

muscular and lean. My nut-brown hair, slicked back from the water, shines. My eyes are clear and brown, with dark lashes forming an exotic line about the edges of the lids.

This is The Dream. I'm free of the thing at last. And I'm handsome, strong, manly. Because of The Dream, this reality is no less real than the default reality I was born into. With a little more will, I could choose to stay. The Dream would suffuse itself into my brain. My original body would die. But this reality isn't my choice. I have many dreams that are so much better. I can take my time to choose.

When I am finished with The Dream, I awaken in my room. The mist snakes about my shoulders, flashing, smelling of sunlight and roses I reach up, grasp it–like grasping a cloud–and settle the device in the box. I shove the box gently into the back of the closet, then go to check on the thing.

It is sleeping, a soft snore escaping its chapped lips. I lean over it and press my palm to its warm forehead. "I'm sorry," I say softly.

It doesn't stir.

*

When I use The Dream again, Edith is alive. She is too beautiful for me to accept; blue eyes, creamy golden skin, slim waist, blonde curls that fall like sunlight about her shoulders. She has the scent of wildflowers. That I am related to her seems impossible. I am flabby and dull next to her. I am awkward and clumsy.

But Edith doesn't think so. She loves me.

"You can be anything, do anything, Ricky," she says. Her smile is reflected inside me. "You're intelligent and compassionate. That combination is rare these days. Beauty can be bought. A tender soul, a gentle conscience, cannot In that, you are more beautiful than anyone in the world."

"You're supposed to say those things to me," I say. "It's your job."

"I wouldn't say them if they weren't true."

"I love you, Mom."

Her slim hand cups the side of my head.

The Dream allows me to experience a whole day condensed to an hour with my mother.

I wake up rested and smiling.

When the thing yells, I go to it with a new strength.

*

The day the doctor comes, the thing is listless and inattentive. It keeps falling asleep, even while she pokes it.

"What's wrong?" I ask.

"Nothing physical that wasn't there already," she answers.

"I've done everything you told me to do, every day. I never leave the house."

She puts a hand on my shoulder to stop me. "I know. You take very good care of him. It's not for lack of care that he's having a bad day. I can see that. Clean sheets, clean house. His hair is combed; he's getting his proper amounts of medication. How has he been otherwise?"

For a moment it's difficult to answer. I have trouble thinking of the thing as "he" or "him." "Depressed," I finally reply. "Irritable. Angry. Usually violent."

The doctor writes on a notepad. She rips off a page. "I'm going to change his medication dosage a little. Here's a new prescription. It's the same thing, but the pills will be more potent."

I nod, taking the paper.

"It should make him more receptive to you, and less violent. Let me know how he does in the next couple of weeks. I may want to change my schedule to fit him in for another examination before the end of the month."

"Thank you," I say.

She looks at me, with her black eyes soft and glimmering, for a long moment. Then she says, "You're doing a great job, Rick."

I shrug.

"A lot of people would turn their backs on a situation like this," she continues. "Turn the case over to the state."

"It … it's not what I want to do," I stammer, glancing sidelong at the thing.

"I know." She smiles with only her eyes and turns away. "If you have any problems, you call. And you still have that list of other numbers I gave you? Just in case you want assistance, or someone to talk to."

I nod.

"Good." She picks up her medical bag, grabs her coat from the chair by the door. "No fee, as usual. And I'll see you again soon. Are you okay?"

"Yes," I say, touching the side of the bed where the thing lies, feeling the stiff press of clean cotton. "Yes."

"All right, then."

I snatch my hand up and step forward. "I'll see you to the door."

*

In The Dream I can relive any situation I want, or create new scenarios to star in. I can be slim, good-looking, and desirable to any woman. I can relive old holidays, or create new ones. I can save the Earth from alien invasion, heal the sick, bring back the dead … I can experience anything, and when I am ready to choose, I can remain there forever. My favorite situation to dream is one in which Mom and Dad are still alive, having narrowly avoided death from the new, unheard-of virus that, in real life, consumed them both like a sudden fever, eating flesh and bone, withering them painfully from the inside out. And I am their son again, not necessarily handsome, not perfect, but well loved.

Tonight The Dream gives off my father's old scent: English Leather and rose wine, printer's ink and Borax. Because this is The Dream, the magazine and newspaper business still flourishes despite laptops and electronic book readers. In the past, in his prime, my father made a good living at his print shop.

The Dream's lights flicker amber, rare lime green and gray. As I hold The Dream, staring into the mist and ever-swirling rainbows, it pulses against my palms, tickling them with what feels like faint electrical charges. I raise my hands to my face. The Dream presses into my nose, eyes, mouth.

I inhale. I am fourteen.

Dad comes into my room, fresh from work, his hands and fingernails gray from too much ink and too much soap. My mood goes from sour to hopeful to ashamed.

"What's this I hear about a fight at school?" he asks me.

I've been crying, so I don't look at him.

"Well?" he prompts.

"Sean called me 'Tubbo' again."

"That all?"

I shrug.

"So, what have I told you in the past? That names don't matter, right? It's what's inside that counts."

I look at him, at his slicked-back black hair caught in a tight tail, at his smooth face and honey skin. I don't look a thing like him. It's hard to believe, sometimes, he's my father, my true, blood father.

"Dad, don't you see how easy that is for you to say? You don't look like me. You've never looked like me. You *don't* know what it's like!"

He sits beside me on the bed. "So you have to hit to defend yourself," he says softly. "You have to lash out, hurt, until the inside and the outside match your view of yourself."

I blink, look down at my lap. My chubby fingers fold together. I hate myself.

"You're not ugly," he continues. "So you don't have to be ugly."

"You don't understand," I repeat, whispering.

"No," he answers. His hand touches the top of my head. I can feel his fingers curve in my hair. "You're right. I don't understand. Because when I look at you, I see what's good and right. I see what's beautiful about human beings. Something rare amid all the destruction of our world. Something different. You've never done me wrong before. Don't start." His hand moves to my shoulder, squeezes.

For a moment I am all he says I am.

For a moment.

I wake on my back. The Dream puddles on my chest, oily, shifting in light and mist.

The thing down the hall is calling. "Food! Food!"

I close my eyes tightly and force myself to take deep breaths.

*

Its one good arm throws its food on the wall. I clean it up.

It urinates on the sheets. I clean it up.

It spits its medicine at me. I clean it up.

"Get me Edith," it demands.

"She's not here."

"I know you're keeping her from me, you idiot, you fat toad, good for nothing ..." The thing thrashes, crying out. It pushes off its covers with its flailing arm. It's cool in the room. I grab the sheet and blanket and cover the thing back up as it screams.

"Get out," it yells. "If you can't bring me Edith, then just get out. And never come back!"

I leave the room as it continues to spit at and curse me.

In my room I remove The Dream from its box.

The Dream remains my only escape from this madness. My chest is tight, my eyes swollen. Reflecting my mood, The Dream in my hands twists and bends. The center becomes devoid of rainbows. A dark tornado appears in the mist. The scent is acrid, like burnt tar.

This isn't what I want.

Even in the privacy of my own room, I can still hear the thing down the hall. It moans and howls for Edith. Wincing, I start to raise my hands and The Dream to my face.

The thing screams in a horrible, high-pitched voice. "Edith!"

My hands stop. I'm breathing hard, trying not to cry. I've had enough. I jump up, balancing The Dream on one hand, and yank open the door.

The hall is dark, but The Dream gutters like a candle lighting the way.

At the end of the hall is the thing's room. With my free hand, I turn the cold metal doorknob.

"Edith?" questions a sobbing voice from within.

I enter the room. The only light is from a lamp by the bed. The thing lies in a mess of covers, its face scarred with tears, its eyes pained, terrified. This is what the virus left me after it killed my mother and father. My mother is dust now. But my father ... Before it left his system–still barely breathing, still pumping blood–it had taken most of his body, most of his mind. The virus changed him from my father to the thing.

"Not Edith!" he says, seeing me come into the room. His chapped lips grimace.

"No, you're wrong." Resigned, I walk slowly towards the bed. Even though the virus took away the father I knew, still, I have never been able to deny him anything. "I've brought her."

"Edith? Here?" he whispers.

"Yes." I move my hand forward and show him the slowly darkening miniature electrical storm that is The Dream. "Edith is here."

Sons of Neverland

lost
in decades of
leaf cities
they will
fall
into our lives
in flickers of dust
the ache of the empty street
will echo their notes
boys of ashen suns
and ghost ships
they will
breathe fog
bring the ice
of sapphire winters
carry the fires of our
lamp-lit hearts
moon-caught
patched and damp-eyed
in the auburn drifts of dusk
the life-spans of stars
will be theirs

The Thin Place

Payne said to me, "I wish I was a nova."

"That's dumb."

"No, it would be the most natural, wonderful thing."

"To burn up? To die in a ball of flame?"

He sunk his hands deep into his pockets. His elbows stuck out like awkward, featherless wings. "Or collapse into a black hole, maybe – an intelligent black hole."

"You're flipped." I watched him kick at a smooth, flat stone, the kind best for skipping on a mirror-still lake. The sole of his tennis shoe flapped, catching dirt.

"I want to live like that, or die trying."

"Live like what?"

Payne tossed back his black hair, the look on his face too old for twelve. "Burning," came his reply.

I didn't tell him that, to me, he'd always burned brighter than the rest of the guys, that it showed in his gold-flecked eyes, in the heat of a look, in the way he stole through the forbidden garden of Mrs. Nausbaum on a double-dog dare like some demon on a provincial path of ruin.

"Angelo?" He was looking at me strangely, that heat of him affecting me, making me nervous yet honored that out of everyone at school he'd picked me for his best friend.

"Yeah?"

"You don't believe me, do you?"

"I believe you." I looked away, my breath catching. "But I still think you're flipped."

"You just wait. Some day I'll figure it all out."

*

The day was one of those orange days of October. The air seemed to ooze with filtered light from overcast skies.

Leaves hung off trees like dangling corpses waiting for an inspired gust to free them.

I was nursing a low-grade fever, missing a second day of work at the microbiology lab because of some stubborn flu bug I'd caught, most likely on my last visit to the dentist. The phone rang.

"Hey, pal. What's up?"

"Hi, Payne. A touch of the flu, I guess."

"Sorry to hear that. I had some spare time and wondered if you wanted to meet me for lunch."

I smiled into the receiver. "Don't you ever work like the rest of us?"

"All the time. Just because I work at home doesn't mean I don't work. You try juggling stock and real estate investments and tell me how much free time you have "

"No, thanks. I'll stick to honest work." I often teased him like that, a little jealous, perhaps, but mostly proud. He played with large sums of money while I played with next to invisible bugs. He owned apartment buildings and condominiums. I owned dozens of jars of multi-celled organisms that resembled little more than mucus globules.

"So, Angelo, are you up for lunch?"

"I'll just pop a few aspirin and be good as new."

"Great. I have something I want to discuss with you. Meet me at noon at the Dark Room."

"Great."

But it wasn't all that great. I felt like hell. But I could never say no to Payne. He was that important to me. And my need to feel some of that importance in return was like a magnet pulling me toward metal.

When we were twelve, I always thought I'd outgrow the intensity I shared with him. Now at twenty-eight I stopped over-thinking it. Analysis only made me homophobic, paranoid about the fact that the few women who'd been in my life had very quickly walked out, while Payne stayed, closer than a brother at times, quietly satisfying.

There was no category for our relationship. No definition. We preferred it that way.

I dressed carefully, as if for a parent, or a date. I put on soft black slacks and a long-sleeved white shirt.

When I walked out of the house the sky looked like a huge specimen of blue-gray mold.

The aspirin still hadn't kicked in.

*

The Dark Room blinded me. My eyes took their time adjusting to the lack of light. Payne's hand on my shoulder was all the evidence I had that I had not stepped off the world and into endless night.

The host wore white. I could see him as a blob of paleness against black as he led us to an empty table.

Candles dotted each tabletop. They swelled and guttered like little stars. Here and there, I could see people's faces, waxen and yellow like dolls waiting for tea in a little kid's playroom.

"This is my favorite place to eat," Payne was saying as we sat. "Everything's perfect."

I blinked and found my napkin, unfolding it on my lap.

"Angelo? You okay?"

"Sure. Just a bit dizzy."

"You know, it really is fortunate you have a fever today."

"What?"

"It'll make it so much easier for you to understand what I have to tell you."

"What?" I repeated. It wasn't like Payne to be so cold.

"I mean that a fever makes a person more vulnerable. Therefore you will be more open to what I have to say." His hair was coming into focus now, not a part of the blackness around us anymore, but a separate glowing entity. He'd let it grow long so that in back it touched the spot between his

80

shoulder blades, while the sides were swept back to reveal the lobes of his ears. Short wisps sprinkled his forehead with haphazard bangs. All of it framed a large, uncharacteristic grin as he stared at me, as I tried to make sense of him and failed.

"Payne? Are you saying you're glad I'm sick?"

"Yes." His grin narrowed. "I mean no. Just listen to me, okay?"

"Uh huh." My mouth was open. I couldn't seem to acquire the strength to close it.

The waiter came and Payne ordered drinks, a beer for himself, and wine for me. I wanted tea but didn't think of it until the waiter was gone.

"What I wanted to say was one of my investment partners, a lady from Japan, shoed me something the other day that I've been looking for all my life. Angelo, you won't believe it. You won't. But I have to show you. It's a major discovery, but the world doesn't know yet. It's not ready to know."

"I don't know what you're talking about."

"Just listen to me. She told me that if I told anyone she would have me destroyed. It was a weak threat, though. She's not that powerful. And I have to tell you, I have to show you. She'll understand. You need to see it, too. I don't know why she chose me, why show showed me, but..."

"Payne, wait, you're babbling. Who is this person and what did she show you?"

"She's from Japan. Older than fuck. Her name is Midori something. I can never remember, let alone pronounce her last name. And what she showed me is...is unbelievable. It's just, well, I have to share it with you."

"Well, what is it?" I was staring at the candle in its amber jar. It made pictures against my eyes of a figure dancing, someone made entirely of fire.

"It's not what, it's where. It's a place."

"A place? You mean like a garden or something?"

"Or something."

The figure in the candle raised her arms as her legs melted into fire, flickering and merging. She moved to the rhythm and flow of whatever patterns the oxygen molecules fed her.

In the flames were dangling leaves and hanged men. A voice said, "And you, sir?"

"Angelo?"

"What" I glanced up, blinking.

"What do you want to eat?"

I looked down, away from the flame, then up again. "Um, toast. That's all."

The waiter wrote it down. He had a ring on his forefinger that sparkled. I noticed my wine had come. Shadows of the fire dancer swirled in it, the tapered glass shimmering, the wine molten gold.

I reached for it, took a sip. It tasted like taco sauce. Swallowing a second sip, I cleared my throat and spoke. "So, that's it. You want to show me a place?"

"That's right." Payne took a gulp of beer. His upper lip glistened. Everything not of the dark glistened.

"Must be special."

"You wouldn't believe it if I told you."

I stared at my wine, at my blunt fingers that caressed the wine-glass base. "I don't know. And what do you mean the world isn't ready for it? Since when do are you a philosopher?"

"I'll take you there after lunch. You'll understand."

"After lunch?" My fingers gripped the smooth glass. "I don't know if I'm up to it. "

"You're perfect." His eyes held mine, fiery. I couldn't say no.

"Payne. I'm sick."

"I know. Like I said. Perfect."

I stared at him. "You're not making any sense."

"Just wait." He shook his hair. It moved around his face like liquid ink. I'd always wanted hair like that. Mine was black, too, but coarse and dull. I felt like a poorer version of him, born incomplete.

Today my brain believed that. It spun weakness. And flame.

I so wanted to be like Payne. He literally blazed.

I said, "All right. I'll go."

I couldn't say no.

*

The house was a single-story with a tiny front yard. The browned grass needed cutting; the parched air needed rain. I thought if I lay down on the ground, or even stepped for just a moment on the stiff, dry blades I'd be soaked up into the fever of the Earth and never released.

Payne touched my elbow, steering me onto the concrete path. "Angelo." His voice seemed cool. My hands were hot. "This way."

A door opened.

Payne, very softly, "I have to show him."

"No." A woman's voice, rich and firm. Payne blocked the door so I couldn't see her.

"Please, he's someone who will understand."

"I show you because I like you," the woman said harshly. Her accent seemed out of place. "I know you man with potential for supernatural talent. I know you may use knowledge well. He not same. Now, go before you disappoint old woman more. You very disappoint me."

"Wait. Midori, but…"

The door slammed.

"Angelo." Payne turned to me. I wavered. "It's incredible. Believe me, you have to see it. You have to." He pounded on the closed door.

I told him, "I believe you," and watched his fist batter the heavy oak structure.

After awhile, Payne stepped back, shaking his head. "We'll get in," he mumbled. "Somehow, we'll get in."

"Inside the house?"

He nodded. "Tonight. We'll come back."

"But she said no."

"We'll break in."

"No way, Payne. It's not worth this. You're flipped."

He whirled, his eyes wet, deep as autumn. "It is worth it," he hissed. "Worth more than you could ever imagine."

My head ached. I could imagine a lot.

I followed him back to the car.

*

I'd fallen asleep on Payne's couch. Now I couldn't remember how I got there.

"Don't worry. You'll see it. I'll get you in."

"What?" I tried to sit up.

Payne stood in front of me. He was dressed in dark jeans and a black sweat shirt. "Please say you'll come with me."

"I can't. I don't feel well at all." My heard throbbed. My skin ached. Payne looked like a shadow-ghost, shimmering in heat. Then his form shortened, closed in on me like smoke. I squinted. He was on his knees. His hand found mine.

"You're my best friend, right?"

I nodded, wincing from the pain in my head.

"This is worth everything to me. Now, I ask, what am I worth to you?"

Though I couldn't believe the question…we didn't talk about these things…I answered nonetheless. "Everything."

"Then come with me."

"All right."

A grin blurred his face. "You never could say no."

84

Smiling hurt.

*

The air took away my warmth. The sky looked solid, like the ceiling of an obsidian cave. I felt trapped and cold.

I avoided the grass, staying on the sidewalk, then on the dirt at the side of the house. But Payne stepped right on it. I could see the lawn trying to grab at his ankles but he didn't seem to notice.

While Payne jimmied open a side window, I leaned against sharp stucco. I was too delirious to be afraid. Or maybe I was too stupid. I leaned and listened to the occasional bird, to cars. Payne's work sounded like a soft saw. Something snapped.

"We're in," he announced. Just then, his arm caught on a bush. Thorns snagged his black sleeve. "Goddamn rosebushes," he cursed.

I could barely breathe as I watched him disentangle himself.

He made me go first, boosting me over the sill where I had a brief war with long, musty curtains. When I felt solid floor against my knees, I rested and waited. It was too dark to see. All I could smell was dust. In my stomach, fear began to uncurl.

Payne's hand fell on my shoulder and I startled. "This way," he said.

"How can you see?" I whispered.

"I know this place."

A door opened and the room brightened. At Payne's feet stretched a hall where phantom light glowed from the far end.

"Where are we going?"

"There." Payne pointed toward what looked like an ordinary door that might lead to an ordinary bedroom.

"It's in there?" I asked.

He nodded, putting a quieting finger to his lips.

I followed him into the hall, my eyes on his hair, my hand gripped in his. When we got to the door he slowly, silently turned the knob. Nothing happened.

"It's locked," he whispered, pulling a thin wire out of his jeans pocket. He worked for several minutes with no luck.

Footsteps clicked by the end of the hall. Payne pushed me back into the first room, closing the door part way. I couldn't see out but I listened. The footsteps thudded louder, then stopped. Payne was holding his breath. I started to count. When I got to fifty, the footsteps came again, this time retreating toward the front of the house.

Payne let out a long breath. "That was close."

"Do you think she heard us?"

"No. She sensed something, though. She's psychic."

I frowned. "Psychic? Really?"

He didn't answer.

Back in the hall, Payne worked on the door. Finally I heard a click. "That's it," he whispered, looking straight at me. "Are you ready?"

I nodded.

He took my hand. "Hold on."

The door swung slowly inward. Still staring at the back of Payne's head, I followed his lead. Something bright flashed in my eyes. I instinctively closed them.

"Beautiful," I heard Payne say. The door snapped shut behind me.

"Open your eyes."

I did, and stumbled.

Fire washed my feet in gold and blue. On all sides, flames spilled toward us. I yelled.

Payne squeezed my hand, steadying me. "Isn't it great?"

My mouth had fallen open. But I couldn't speak.

Payne didn't wait for an answer. "Listen to me. Now you can understand. This is a tiny dimension just around the

86

bend from ours. It exists in the middle of a collapsing star. But the star is on another plane. It may not look like you're standing on solid ground, but you are. It's just crystal clear. The reason we're not blinded is because the dimension barriers dim the light enough so we can look at it. Midori told me that."

Fire surrounded us, but there was not the expected intense heat. My eyes filled. "It's a trick," I said slowly. "You're making fun of me because I'm sick."

Payne let go of my hand and moved forward. "Superstitious people call areas like these thin places. Like fairy rings or something."

I stumbled again, almost fell.

"Look. Look at this. Remember what I told you once when we were kids? This is what I wanted to experience. And I told you I'd find a way. Well, here it is. And it's real, Angelo. As real as our world, just different. And very, very small. It's about the size of a normal bedroom, actually. I've tried to walk as far as I can. After about five steps I'm back by the door."

I turned, but saw no door, only a fountain of fire. "The door's gone. Where is it? Where?"

"It's there," Payne said. "You just have to feel for it."

I did just that. When I found the knob I turned it experimentally. It didn't move. "I can feel the door," I called over my shoulder. "But it won't open." I turned toward him.

His eyebrows rose. "It won't?"

"You try."

Payne worked at it for many minutes with his wire before facing me. He wet his lips. His brown eyes flared. I thought of the dancing girl in the candle in the Dark Room.

Payne forced a smile. "I guess we'll have to wait until someone lets us out."

"No one knows we're here."

"Midori sensed it. She'll let us out."

But I remembered what he'd said about her telling him that she'd destroy him if he ever gave away her secret. I sat down hard.

Our bubble in the middle of the star was small and frightening. But nor now I felt no fear Instead, I had to smile at Payne's realization of his so preposterous dream.

"I'm sorry, Angelo," he said softly. "She'll come. I know she will."

My eyes stung as I nodded. "It's beautiful. Thank you for bringing me here."

After awhile, Payne sat, his back to me, his hair glowing vermillion.

For a long time, neither of us spoke.

Then Payne said, "I'd jump into it if I could."

I nodded. "To die by fire. You always wanted that." My eyes stared, hypnotized, into the middle of an oily, blue-orange conflagration. I couldn't look away. It occurred to me that to sit in the middle of another dimension, watching a sun burn out while discussing forms of suicide was completely insane. We were waiting to die, but still I wasn't afraid.

I closed my eyes, then opened them. The dancer from the candle reappeared, body orange and red, arms tapering to yellow, her legs formed by blue. "Do you see that?" The question was out before I could stop myself.

"What?" Payne turned, his face a dark profile.

"It looks like a woman dancing in the flames." I hunched my shoulders. The admission sounded foolish.

"I've been watching her for several minutes now," Payne answered quietly.

"She's a pretty illusion."

"Yeah."

I looked down. Swirling fires fought between my legs. I thought I saw a face. Several faces.

"Payne?"

"Yeah?"

"They're everywhere. People. In the fire."

"I thought it was just me." He turned and his face looked like a burning demon's. "You see them, too." He shook his head. "I don't understand it."

Pretty faces with flares bursting around them like bronze, liquid curls seemed to push up at me. I put my hand to the floor as if to touch one of them and pain shot through me.

"Ouch!" I jumped up, almost falling as my sluggish brain tried to assimilate a change of balance.

Payne stood quickly. "What is it?"

"Something burned me. Look." I held out my hand. Blisters had begun to form on the palm.

Payne placed his palm underneath mine, staring at my burnt skin as if he'd never seen anything like it.

"What if these walls aren't stable?" I asked suddenly. "What if something or someone can reach through them, reach through to us?"

He looked up. "I don't know."

Just then an arc of white light, like lightning, juggled above our heads. A scent of ozone singed the air.

"Payne!" I hunched deeper into myself but was afraid to sit. Instead, I stood with my arms wrapped around my chest, the pain in my hand forgotten.

"I don't understand." Payne took a step away from me.

"What's happening?"

"I don't know."

Another zigzag of light slapped the air.

"Payne?"

"Something really bad is happening."

I closed my eyes. The brightness of the room flowed into the dark of my mind.

To die by fire is the best way to go. I kept telling myself that, but my whole body shook. I could feel moisture trying to push from between my tightly closed eyelids.

The next moment, something struck me. A thousand needles simultaneously invaded my skin. I tried to call out but my mouth wouldn't open.

Then I tasted ash.

And I knew it was over.

*

Far away, in another infinity, another continuum, a phone was ringing.

Something sharp pressed into one side of my tongue. The pain subsided as I inhaled hard. It was like a first breath, a startled awakening from nothing into existence.

I opened my eyes. The white walls of my room swirled, then floated together into solid, tall barriers. The first image I sought was the digital clock. Eleven-thirty A.M.

But what day?

The phone rang again, and I jerked at the loud noise. I reached for the bed stand and lifted it.

"Yo, Doc Angelo." It was my co-worker Pat from the lab.

"Hi, Pat."

"You coming into work today? Those fungi of yours are taking over the fridge."

"Um, tomorrow. I'll be in tomorrow."

"Anything I can do for you? You sound wonked."

"Thanks, no. I just need rest."

"Sure thing, Doc. I'll baby-sit the mold."

"Thanks." I hung up and tried to sit. The room spun. That's when I remembered I should have been dead.

*

Payne wasn't answering his phone. The drive to his place was short. Aspirin helped keep reality in focus.

By the time I reached the front door of his house, I had a strong hunch I was in the wrong place. The car out front wasn't his, and the yard was full of roses. Payne hated roses. But I knocked anyway.

An old woman opened the door.

"Who are you?" The words were out before I realized how rude they sounded.

I might ask same," she replied, her accent thick, though her pronunciation was precise. I'd heard the voice before. Turning away with a soft apology, I started down the porch steps. But just before she closed the door, I looked back. "Excuse me, Ma'am, but is your name Midori?"

"How you know this?"

My jaw dropped. "Do you now a man named Payne?"

"Payne my gardener?"

"Your gardener?"

"He come Thursdays. Is Saturday today."

"Oh. Yes. Thank you."

I almost ran to my car.

As I drove to where I thought the old woman's house really was, I noticed that autumn hadn't quite yet developed. I remembered yesterday the leaves were brittle as burnt paper crumbling off branches that could no longer sustain them. And the sky had been a rotten gray. Today it was as clear blue as a shallow lake.

I pulled up in front of a yellowed, old house, the one Payne and I had sneaked into the night before. My hands were shaking as I stepped into the street and walked around my car. I told myself this was all a ridiculous fantasy, a fever dream I would awaken from and later forget.

Before I reached the front walk, the door opened and a man with short black hair stepped out. He had a beer in one hand, a TV Guide in the other. "Hey, Angelo. What brings you over today?"

"Payne?"

"What's a'matter?"

Gone was the shine in his black hair, the sultry glow in his eyes, the bounce in his step.

"What happened to you?" I asked.

"Me? Nothing much. Why? Do I look like hell?" He grinned, but it was a forced, painful grimace that pulled at his face like a curse.

My heart thumped hard against my chest and side. "Uh, no."

"Come on in for awhile. The wife's gone for the day. I don't know where. The kids are around somewhere."

"Wife?"

He hiccupped. "Oh, how quickly we forget. But then Darla isn't that memorable, huh? I often ask myself, how did I get stuck with her?"

"Darla," I mumbled.

"Come on in, have a beer." He led me into a small, dark living room. We sat on a low couch where a muted TV flashed a college football game. My headache started to come back. I ignored the beer Payne handed me and simply stared.

"So, what's been happening with you?" Payne asked.

"Uh, not much." I set the beer on the coffee table. "But I meant to ask you if you remember anything strange happening last night."

He frowned, his eyes half-closed, tired. "Last night? No. Why?" He scratched absently at his chest.

"Just curious."

"Come to think of it, I did have this really strange dream. You just reminded me. There were fire fairies in it. You know, like little people made out of fire. They were intelligent, I think. That's all I remember. Strange, huh?"

"Fire fairies?"

He nodded. "Yep. Maybe I had too much to drink."

I clasped my hands in my lap to keep them from trembling. "Do you remember when we were kids and you said you wanted to be a nova? Or die like one?"

"What?"

"Do you remember that?"

He looked at me as if I were a stranger. Then he shook his head. "Nah. I don't remember."

I felt my eyes start to sting.

"Hey, pal, you all right?" he asked.

"Sure. Can I use your john?"

"You know where it is."

I blinked, got up slowly and walked out of the room without looking back. When I entered the hall I knew where I was headed.

The door looked the same. I put my hand on the cold, metal knob. It wasn't locked and turned easily, swinging inward. For a moment I shut my eyes, unable to look.

When I opened them I saw an ordinary entrance to an ordinary bedroom.

Behind me I heard footsteps. "Angelo?" Are you lost?"

My vision blurred. "Yes."

A chill hand touched mine. "You're burning up. Come on, pal. The bathroom's this way."

I closed the door. Where Payne stood, a cold world waited.

Dusk, Moon, Starlight

Dusk
  a gold ship ripples
  sky's edge
  scarlet leaves fall upon
  lost cities

Moon
  torn cloud
  runaway wind
  the old glow
  of gray ice

Starlight
  a sage-burnt horizon
  flowering
  embers of secret futures
  unrisen

The Beautiful People

The beautiful people were out that night, restless, cruel-edged but looking oh so good in the moonlight and the streetlight and the golden beams of the bar where the polished wood counters stretched on forever.

I polished those counters. Often. Too often. Until they gleamed and showed me my own unwanted reflection, pudgy, white cheeks dusted unevenly with a twelve-hour beard, dark crisp hair that would never lay flat, bloodshot eyes, neck too skinny, too long. And yet, as I looked, I realized the softness that was me, that countenance of rare masculine honesty, hadn't left, and I vowed it never would. I did not want to become the hardened dolls these other people dreamed of being. I did not need a semblance of beauty to learn about my own heart.

And yet, how could I not be drawn by it?

On stage the band played, Elvis on Velvet. Great name for a band, I thought. The drummer wore the rhinestones. The bass player had the dark, pumped up Elvis bangs. And the lead singer had Elvis's voice.

That night there were so many of them out dancing, shimmying through the night, drunk. Those beautiful people calculating, showing off, searching. And all, every one of them, unnatural. I could tell by the eyes. Women in spangled dresses slit up to their tail bones. Men with transcendent suntans and biceps that threatened to split the sleeves of their shirts. It seemed no one – no one! – was left who hadn't been through the trauma. Except…

Tam was singing, Elvis-voice full of remote places: grottoes filled with green light, echo-frozen tundra, an African sky gorged on thunder. They were all good. Tam was great.

And when I looked at his eyes, I could see he was a natural. No sharpness there. No cruel demons haunting the deep brown depths. Lean, tall, skin like coffee that shone, supple but strong. Thick black hair rippling along his scalp where he'd slicked it back, ends hanging coarse yet gleaming on his shoulders.

The noise level was a pulsing screech, punctuated by booms. You could barely hear the words to the song. "Everything is just a dream…in a broken voice I say I love you…"

His big eyes met mine over the din, the smoke, the flailing hands, the rocking heads. My lips parted. My skin prickled. It was as if at that moment I stood outside myself, watching myself respond to him. Watching the rare language that can happen between two people when there are no words.

That night, when everything had seemed so hard-edged and the shared world of fake beauty completely eluded me, Tam noticed me. Me.

And after the set when I brought him and the other band members – all of them fakes but Tam – free drinks, he stopped me with that shimmering voice of his. "Sit for a minute."

I put the tray in my lap, feeling awkward. Stupid. The big room became small; the ceiling fans eight feet overhead threatened to cut into my already hacked, coarse hair. I wasn't shy. I was a bartender. But Tam made the moths in my stomach hatch.

Not just that night, but all the nights after. Again and again.

The other band members wandered off. Tam leaned in. "You don't go in for this crowd at all, do you?"

I shook my head.

"I'm not like them, you know."

I nodded. "I know." My nervous voice slipped high, then low.

"You like my singing?"

I nodded again.

"Good. Cause you have to if we're gonna be friends." His dark hand touched my knee through my pants. Sweat broke out across my back.

When we went backstage where it was quiet and we could really talk, he said, "You fascinate me because you haven't done it. Gone through the treatment, made yourself like all the rest. That makes you exotic. That makes you a mystery."

In a way, he was saying he noticed my ugliness. He hadn't had the treatment because he was already beautiful. What was my excuse?

And yet, he'd noticed me.

Speechless, I could only smile. And then he stepped forward and his lips burned that smile onto my face so that nothing mattered anymore, only him and me, that night when the polished counters seemed to go on forever and the beautiful people all thought they had it made in the moonlight and the streetlight as they banned all shadows while I held the real thing in my arms. All their beauty can't make them know it's this kind of honesty that makes your heart swell and break. Makes you soar. Makes you a god.

Two weeks later, Tam and I moved in together.

*

"Noah," Tam said, as we lay together in bed, three A.M., soaking up the dark. "Really, I want to know, why'd you never do it?"

"Go for the treatment, you mean?" I held him and his skin was polished heat slicked to mine. "It's not an easy decision, you know."

"Oh, I know. Frankly, I think kids these days are agreeing to go through with it too easily. And the adults aren't setting a good example. All that pain and suffering for looks. Only looks. What about the insides?"

"Yeah. But you never had to face the mirror and scowl, I bet," I said, all too aware now of the light paunch of my stomach that didn't go at all well with the rest of my frail looks. And my hair felt like one big mat stuck to my head. And everywhere he gleamed perfect and hardened, I felt myself sag.

"But Noah, don't you know we all do? No one's satisfied, even if they're nothing wrong with how they look. It's how we're taught. I used to look at myself and think maybe if I was white I'd be more handsome. Or maybe if my hair were straight..."

"You?" It was hard to believe. My beautiful Tam, not satisfied. He was only twenty, though. I'd learned that the first night. And not even that experienced in bed for someone so outgoing. His naiveté had not yet taken into account the accumulated fat of age, the gray and the wrinkles. Yeah, barely out of his teens, he was still immortal youth, beauty engraved forever on pure, untarnished night.

"Sure," he finally answered after too long silent. "There's things I'd want to correct about myself."

"Like what?" I laughed. I felt him draw away and a pang of empathy shot through my gut. "Wait," I said. "You said you didn't buy into it all."

"I don't. But you've seen my feet. They're way too big. And my shoulders...they could be broader. And my eyes...they're a little too far apart. And well, hell, while we're at it, the myth about big hands and big feet just ain't true. I could do with a thicker coc..."

I covered his mouth with my palm, the gesture almost a slap. Then I moved over him, holding him tight, my lips replacing my hand. When I pulled away, I said, "You're perfect. You hear me? You're perfect." And I began to make love to him to prove it.

But there was a panic in me the touching could not ease. I was afraid I would lose him. It was, after all, that kind of a world.

*

When the treatments became available to the general public at affordable prices, I was ten years old. The controversy at that time was not about the nature of weighing looks against intelligence, vanity against wit. No. It was about how to regard those who chose not to have the treatments, those who chose to stay plain, or fat, or big-nosed, or small-breasted. "We should not look down on these people," said spokespersons from treatment centers around the world. "We should just try to embrace them until they come around."

But coming around wasn't as easy as it sounded. The treatments took three months and had to be repeated every seven years for the rest of your natural life. And the treatments were very painful. In effect, you were choosing to be ill for three long, agonizing months in exchange for muscles, tans, smooth faces, long-lashed eyes, bright and streaming hair. Nano-bugs crawled around inside you and did the work. And there was no drug that could cure the pain. Most people spent those three months screaming and wailing until it was done. They became sleep-deprived, haunted by nightmares of torture, and in the end, when they came out if it, the scars showed nowhere but in the eyes.

I noticed this when I was very young. Their eyes. The resentment burned there, yet no one ever talked about it. And there was a rigid cruelty that came of the experience, a wiping out of innocence, of any soft compassion that might encompass anyone outside their own mirrors.

There was no proof the process changed your personality. Yet it appeared that way. I saw it first hand. With my sister.

Tam either couldn't or wouldn't understand. "I don't see how," he said one day, "you could be sure it was the treatment that made her kill herself. You said she'd been treated for depression before. You can't blame someone else for that." He was sitting in the living room, the afternoon light making him look dark as loam. His white t-shirt rode up on his flat belly. He strummed a minor key on his guitar.

Fifteen years ago, but it still felt like yesterday. I still heard Kara scream sometimes, an echo of time playing tricks, as if she still lay in bed in the room next to mine growing more and more beautiful with every passing week.

I was afraid for Tam. He said, "They say people forget pain. Women in childbirth can't recall it. People who are injured or sick remember healing, remember the incident, but they don't remember how it actually felt, not really."

I frowned at him.

"No, really. Test it. Do you have any memory of being hurt? In your childhood, maybe, a broken arm or leg…"

"My leg. I fell out of a tree when I was seven."

"I bet you screamed," Tam said. He strummed another minor key.

"Yeah."

"Oh, yeah. But can you remember the actual pain itself? Hmm?"

I thought I could, but it was a lie. A trick of the mind. Tam was right. I saw the doctors from my child perspective pulling on the leg, touch, probing. I remember crying. I remember my mother promising me ice cream when they were through, her nervous hands clutching her purse, her voice trembling. "That's a brave boy. Very brave." I didn't remember the pain.

Tam nodded understanding.

"Okay," I said. "Maybe you're right." It was hard for me, still, to think of my sister. I'd found her, arms sliced, bathtub filled with tepid, red water. Her golden, waist-length hair had been artfully draped over the porcelain sides of the tub. Her full breasts kept pointing up. Her long legs folded against the bottom of the tub like those of a broken doll. I winced the image away.

"Maybe you're right," I conceded again. "But it's still not worth it. All that pain. It couldn't have helped. And the final beauty didn't cure her. Inside, she hadn't changed. She was still unhappy." I blinked suddenly, overcome. I turned away.

"Yeah," Tam agreed.

"So that's my point. The treatment is stupid. I thought you agreed with me about that."

Tam set his guitar aside, got up. "I do." He approached me, put his arms around me from behind.

"Then why were you defending it? Why are you arguing with me?"

"I'm not. It's just that you can't blame the treatment for your sister's problems. Or the world's, either."

I remained silent. The world *had* changed. But I didn't want to talk about it anymore.

*

Tam and I got married that year. An outdoor ceremony. All natural. The trees red and yellow with autumn. The grassy field where we stood crisp with the leaves. My mother came, looking twenty-one and haunted. I felt the post-treatment coldness from her. My father, who'd died when I was a baby, would never have approved of this, she told me with a laugh. But the legalities of same-sex marriage had freed everyone a bit. I liked *that* change in the world. The hang-ups people had when my parents were kids had gone the way of the dinosaurs. The way of ugliness.

But later, she did take me aside and ask me when I was going for my treatment. "I know, I know, I always taught you looks don't really matter, but when you have a choice, why wouldn't you choose to look good?" Her young gaze was brittle, cool, her voice devoid of love. She hadn't been like that before the treatment.

I tried not to feel out of place in my ill-fitting tux, and always fighting my disobedient hair.

The band played. Tam sang a song he'd written just for me. "I love you down the days, past dreaming and beyond." It was sentimental. I loved it. His tux fit him perfectly. His only comment when we'd left the house was, "Aside from my big feet, we make a great couple." He was joking, I thought. He had to be. Inferior as I was to him in appearance, he never made a single comment about me. Only himself. And because he didn't seem disturbed by my drabness, my plainness, I believed her wasn't taken in by the beautiful people and their new grasps on life.

We were in love. What could interfere with such power? We exchanged gold rings. We exchanged our hearts. Nothing else mattered.

*

It became more and more obvious to me that Tam really was dissatisfied with himself when he spent extra time in the bathroom with his glistening hair, or at the gym working out. He became increasingly irritated at his clothing, which was all lovely, and which fit him well. But there was always something wrong. Something he didn't like. Something slightly 'off'.

One night I came home from the bar to find the house a complete mess. It was Tam's one free night of the week. He told me he was going to relax, watch TV, get drunk. Instead, he'd spent the evening cutting up his clothes, bashing in every mirror we owned, and burning his size thirteen shoes in the fireplace. He was prodding the embers with the fire poker, naked, his back to me when I entered the living room.

"Don't look at me," he said.

I came around to face him, knelt. "But I love looking at you." I couldn't tell him how it made *me* feel, my imperfect face, hair, body, and him doing all this because of *his* appearance. This unhappiness: how could it come from something so unimportant?

But that was not the world we lived in. All Tam's fellow band members were hard-eyed from the treatment. Everyone we knew, our friends, our relatives, had been re-sculpted, carved into the haunted beauties, made into survivors of the three-month trauma. Couldn't he see that we had the better deal?

I pulled him into my arms. He didn't let me at first, fighting to back away, appalled at my touch.

"You're uncomfortable with me?"

"But not because of you," he said suddenly, realizing finally that I might be offended. "It's not you. It's me."

After awhile he let me take him into the bedroom. The next day we replaced all the mirrors and got him all new clothes. He swore he'd never let it happen again, the drinking alone part. He made that his excuse; he'd gotten drunk and could think about nothing all night but his damned flaws. That thinking had gotten out of hand.

I still didn't see the flaws myself. I loved him, but that wasn't why I didn't see them. He was beautiful. One of the lucky natural borns who didn't need nano-doctors to spice him up. But I feared the future more than ever after that. If the small things were a problem to him, what would he feel as he grew older and less perfect in a world where old-looking people were more and more scarce, and twenty-one was the physical age of the day?

*

I polished the counter tops under the lights. The counter tops that went on forever and showed me my imperfect face everywhere I wiped. The ceiling fans whooped. The bar was about the open. Everything glittered, ready. Tam was going to sing.

There was a sound test. Blips of electronic noise. The drummer counted "one, two, three" in a bored tone. Away from the mike, a voice called out, "Where's Bigfoot?"

Someone else answers, "Haven't see him, Kirem. Ask Noah."

I stood stunned as Kirem, the bass player, came from backstage, hopped gracefully over the stair and walked toward me. "Hey," he said gruffly. "Tam come with you?"

I came out from behind the bar, put down my rag. When Kirem got close enough, I pulled my arm back, aimed high and caught him in his perfect hard eye with my fist.

Kirem squealed, went down on one knee. "Wha...?"

"Don't you ever call him that again," I said quietly. Then I turned and picked up my rag. My glance caught gleaming dark arms, a golden vest – Tam's favorite – and an amber pendant dangling from a silk cord. I looked up. Tam stood not twelve feet away, face frowning in confusion. He'd just come through the door.

I didn't speak.

Kirem said, "Sorry, man. Tam never said anything about not liking his nickname."

Tam stared at me.

I said, "I've never heard you use that nickname before."

"Well," Kirem said, "you don't hang out with us, so why would you?" He rubbed at his eye, stood and strode back to the stage mumbling, "It's gonna be black and blue, I just know it. I just know it."

Tam sidled up to me. I thought he was going to thank me. He came close. I could smell honeysuckle on him. My heart pumped a little faster. I started to reach out to him. But he pushed me away, saying, "What's the matter with you, dammit!"

He moved away quickly toward the stage, not giving me time to reply.

Stunned, I went into the back room, into the bathroom, and turned on the water. The soap was thick and pink on my

104

hands. I washed my fingers methodically, busying myself with that simple ritual as if the soap could chase away all discomfort, distress, even love. Finally, I looked up. The mirror over the sink was water-spotted, and the image there little better. My perpetually blood-shot, watery blue eyes filled with tears as I answered Tam's question out loud. "Nothing's wrong with me. I'm the same I always was. The same."

The only reply was the gurgle of water journeying they drain. I sighed, dried my hands, then went back into the fray.

*

Our bedroom was dark. We sat on the bed letting the night breeze blow across our bodies from the open window. The moon caught a swatch of Tam's stomach, the mocha skin turning to marble under the ghostly light. An angle caught the soft whiteness at my waist, turned it to a patch of runny cream.

"It's the way I let off steam," Tam explained. "Complaining about my looks. It doesn't mean anything. I only do it with you because you understand. I thought I could say anything to you and have you understand."

"You can," I said. I wanted him to be himself with me. But I also didn't want him to be unhappy.

"Well, then, why would you think Kirem calling me Bigfoot would bother me? I don't care. I mean, I'll complain to you about my big feet, but that's because sometimes I do care. And then you're there for me, always stable, always bringing me back to sanity."

"But if that bothers you…"

"How many times do I have to tell you it doesn't?"

But I remembered all those size thirteen shoes burning. He must have sensed that memory in my silence.

"I told you I was drunk that night. I barely knew what I was doing!"

"But if you feel that way, what you must think of me..."

"What? You're the best, Noah. God, I love you. Don't you know that?"

"But when you look at me..."

"When I look at you I see a real person. The best person I've ever known, someone not taken in by labels or flaws or beauty or whatever. That's why I was so surprised when you hit Kirem. You of all people..."

"I was defending you."

"But I wasn't in need of defending."

Nothing I could say to that. My awkwardness remained. Tam's feelings about his own inadequacies transferred to me. It couldn't be helped. I only wanted him to be happy. If that meant preparing for the day he would give in and take the treatment, then so be it. For that day *would* come. I knew it. I couldn't let him down by disapproving or denying my support. I couldn't stand the thought of leaving him or losing him. But would I be able to look at him, those lacquered brown eyes distant and cool, face hardened to replace his more natural, human-born beauty, and still know him as Tam, love him, pretend we were equals in life and spirit?

A surge of affection for him rose up from my belly and nearly choked me. I turned in the bed and took him in my arms. The moonlight tangled over our bodies.

*

Tam came out of the bedroom stomping. "Just look at this!"

I glanced up from the couch, put down the papers of his new song lyrics I'd been reading. They were good, all of them. Love songs, rants against death and destruction, passionate tragedies of vanity defeating innocence. "What?" I asked.

106

"Just look!" He pointed to his head. "My hair. It won't stay down."

He'd gelled it as usual, and it looked fantastic, that wet-curly style, wild and subdued at the same time. "Looks fine to me," I said.

"It's not falling right." He huffed, pouted. I almost laughed. He scowled at my smirk and went back into the bedroom. I heard a crash.

I closed my eyes, counted to five to calm myself, then got up to see what he'd broken this time.

It was the lamp base, glazed black and a gift from my mother on our wedding. "Tam...," I began.

"Shut up." He was sitting on the edge of the bed, elbows on his knees.

I felt completely helpless. Here he was, one of the most beautiful people I'd ever known, natural or fake, and he still wasn't satisfied. "But Tam, you look fine."

"You don't understand. It's not about that."

"What then?"

"It's the fucking competition! With performing and all that, people have certain expectations. The rest of the band can wake up beautiful. I feel like I have to keep up with them. That pisses me off."

So, I thought, the day I dreaded was coming sooner than I had predicted. I tried not to think about it, him suffering for something he already had, for perfection that didn't really exist except in the minds of those who'd bought into the newer world order and status of beauty. And what would I do? Plain as always, scared of being any other way, I'd sit by his side during the long months and wipe the fevers from his brow as I watched the man I married change into a Tam-doll so he could be like everybody else.

I should have known it when our eyes first met, like everything else in this world, it was too good to be true. I cleared my throat, took a deep breath. "You want it, then. The treatment."

He looked up at me, frowning. "What?"

"Say it. I know you want it. You're always telling me you want to be able to say anything to me. So admit it."

"But..."

I interrupted. "You can't tell me you haven't thought of it, wondered, fantasized. You know you have. Your talent gets you attention on stage, but your looks do, too. You can admit it."

"I do admit that. But I'm just frustrated. That's all."

"But you have wondered, considered the treatment, haven't you?"

"Hasn't everyone?" he asked, eyes wide, unblinking.

I couldn't look at him anymore. It would break me. Tam would break me and the fall was going to be hard. Instead of answering him, I walked from the room.

Getting ready for work that evening, I avoided the mirrors. I knew what I would see. Pudgy face and stomach, skinny legs and arms and neck. Eyes stung with red-shots. Dirty brown hair like carded wool and receding at the temples. I had a rough patch of skin on my neck from shaving that always itched. My clothes were too loose in the ass, too tight at the waist. I looked gangly and out of shape. Wonderful. Just wonderful.

That night Tam came onto the stage stunning as ever, his voice drenched in echoes of night thunder and ancient dead seas and bottomless caves of phosphor. I knew and he knew he must never let that get away from him.

That was when I understood what had to be done.

*

Tam was late getting home. I lay in our bed waiting. He'd been out with his band celebrating as they often did after a performance. I heard the front door close and lock, his soft footsteps on the carpet, the ringing on the table as he set down his keys.

108

Honeysuckle. I could smell it strong and cloying. Tam's aftershave which I loved. But now it threatened to turn my stomach.

He entered the room a shadow, a former fellow visionary, anti-utopist.

"Hey, you awake?" he whispered.

For a moment I couldn't speak. Then I managed one word. "Tam."

I saw him go toward the lamp, replaced after he'd broken it, identical to the one my mother had given us. You couldn't even tell it was a different lamp.

"No," I said, swallowing hard, the tears forming. It hurt to try to speak. Everything hurt. "Don't turn on the light."

"Why?"

I inhaled sharply, grit my teeth, but the pain rattled through me so hard, so long, I couldn't hold back the moan.

Even as Tam heard me, he switched on the light. "What's wrong? Are you sick?" He clamped his mouth shut when he saw me, then a slow look of horror transformed the softness of his face into a visage of despair. "Oh no," he said. "What've you done?"

"For you," I said. "I did it for you."

"No," he said. "You misunderstood. That's never what I wanted for you or for me."

For three months, as he took care of me, I had to look at the disappointment and grief on his face. I had to live with the agony of the nano-bugs as well as the guilt for not trusting him more.

When I was able to function, I went back to work at the bar. I polished the wooden counters until they gleamed, counters that stretched on forever.

Tam continues to sing with that velvet voice of his, private lyrics no longer for me. I have seven years of offers and compliments and consensual societal approval to endure before he might love me again. I don't know if I'll survive.

The Fallen Months

September:
she is made of the terrible fruits of
red suns going down
broken moons leaving glass and crystal
pathways to space
her raincoat sewn from silver ghosts
still howling

October:
in the dew-ice he trembles
my love of the hour of flickering eyes
what moves past the moon is
unexplainable and draculean
all the dusks echo with
worried winds and wings

November:
in your suit of starlight
through your damp trees
you promise
a glimpse of gold cities
someone is running through the soft hills
of acorns and leaves

December:
where the streets turn to black satin
where harbingers go
where we become sleep-tossed
in our flannel beds
where snow gondolas glide
where the long blue night
walks alone

The Texture of Stars

The Powers That Be used to send technicians into space, an occasional scientist. All that came of it were boring lectures and the ability to repair busted satellites. But they fixed that 80 years ago. Now they send Heroes.

The definition of a Hero is less flattering than the generic term. We're expendable, we're highly sexed, and we're stupid. Most of us are failed artists with nothing left to lose. I am a lazy, bad poet who loves to gaze into space. Who better to send off to other worlds? With us, there is the element of drama without the fear of losing some brain valuable to society.

When the PTB signed me up, they changed my name from Weldon Philbert to Stirling Kane, paid for a trip to the most famous flesh-carving institute, Scat Fat, where 50 pounds of excess flab were removed, and bought me a whole new Spandex-leather wardrobe. PTB promised to publish all the bad poetry I wrote out there in space if I turned out to be worthy entertainment.

Now, with twenty-five years of experience and 53 missions behind me, I'm famous. I command my own ship, and everyone who works for me is a Hero, too.

Lacrosse houses eight. I sit at her helm and don't do much, since everything is micro-supercomputerized these days. I stare a lot at the stars. It's a part of my job, and I'm paid very well for it, thank you.

This mission we're off to Jupiter for hydrogen samples and I can think of no ship better qualified than mine for the task. Since Jupiter has no solid surface, we won't be landing. But then, you knew that. It doesn't take a scientist to understand those dynamics. Though fifteen other missions have probed that stormy world, no one has ever gone as close to the planet as we will. Our low altitude probe, complete with diamond-headed bore, is supposed to dive deeper and faster than any other. If it hits solid mass, it will drill. Compressed hydrogen, I'm told by the computer, can be a bitch. Beneath that, someone in the PTB department is hoping to hit rock, and subsequently strike it rich. Diamonds, maybe? Hiding there since the beginning, when our solar system stirred and flared?

"I doubt it," Danielle Blacque tells me when I pose the theory to her over a dehydrated-just-add-water lunch.

I blink and then lean forward dramatically. I can't help but flirt with her. Not only is it in this voyage's job description to do so – the more sex we have on these trips, the more recordings of our journey the PTB can sell to the masses – I love sex almost as much as the stars. Unfortunately, she's never been interested in anyone but her brother, Drac, who happens to interest me, too, but it's only been a month in space so far and I'm trying to save the best for last.

"There's nothing but iron in the center of that planet, if there's anything," she replies, ducking her head to avoid my kiss. She pokes at the damp mash on her plate. After all these years of advancements, human beings still cannot make decent fare for long-voyaging that doesn't look like tie-dyed toothpaste.

"How do you know?" I ask.

"Because I read up on it." Her pale blue eyes roll, the long lashes shadowing her cheek.

"Oh."

"This mission is just a waste of time and money," she adds out the corner of her beautiful mouth.

"Never!" I argue, staring at her breasts through the sheer, red tapestry of her brassiere. She is also wearing designer PTB red lace leggings and nothing more. It's a wonder I don't just shoot myself out an airlock and end this torture.

"I know. I know, we do it for the love of the stars," she says.

"You sound like you're becoming disillusioned."

She shrugs.

My groin tightens against my tight leather bodysuit.

"Maybe I am," she says.

When she leaves I sit there for awhile and stare at the sloping, silver bulkheads.

This is going to be a long four months.

*

In the playroom I lose myself in a live-mystery simulation. A young boy on a Martian satellite colony has just been murdered. It's my job to chase down the suspects. I have too many choices to keep track of, and my attention span has always been short, one of the reasons I became a poet and not a novelist. But it's fun anyway. I get easily side-tracked by virtual hot fudge sundaes and a willowy young girl born in space whose heart would burst if she ever set foot on Earth. She's like a bird in my arms, her bones brittle and light. The half-grav of the satellite is almost too much for her as my body pushes hers against the velvet cover of her bunk. She's a rarity, now that the new ships have their own Earth-like artificial gravities, and a sweet tenderness wells that I've never felt before. Just as I get to the point of wishing away our clothes, the computer image wavers.

"You have failed to track the next clue in the time allotted," a whispery, androgynous voice from beyond the frozen scene. The girl in my arms shimmers, a warm mirage fading to clear air. "Nod for retry. Tilt left for abort."

After failure with Danielle, and now, having just wasted two hours of sleuthing only to have my reward wiped from memory, I am feeling none too rational. I do neither. This is the second time this game has done this to me. I rip off the headset and fling it across the room. It hits Armstrong Vaughn hard in the crotch.

"Oops." I slide out of the stim-chair just as he's removing his own headband. He stares at me, dark brows meeting in a frown.

"What?" he says, picking up my unit from his lap. "You mad at me?"

"Sorry, it just flew right out of my hands."

"Well, Captain, I think you're taking these games a little too seriously." His voice is deep, like chamber music.

"There're only three things I take seriously."

"Me, too." White teeth flash against dark pink lips. "The stars, life, and…"

"Want to discuss it further in my quarters?"

"You *are* desperate," he replies.

*

Armstrong Vaughn takes me into his mouth with a powerful, wet suction. I've had sex with him three times on this voyage, and he's always a lot of fun. But my thoughts are on Danielle as my fingers weave through his many, tiny braids.

We fuck in all sorts of positions for about an hour before we drop, exhausted, into mutual puddles of sweat.

"Have you heard the latest rumor?" he asks, still gasping. His fire-dark eyes gleam.

With my cheek pressed against his warm, outstretched hand, I ask, "Which one?"

"Well, I heard from Hunter who heard it from Sigourney. They say someone on board is a scientist masquerading as a Hero. Supposedly Sig overheard it Earthside at the bon voyage festival. This plot's definitely not in the job description."

"This is the first time I've heard it," I say. I sit up and scoot back to lean against a heated metal bulkhead. From here, the view over my bunk and out the porthole is a treasure trove. The texture of stars is silken; it makes the bulkheads glow.

Armstrong turns onto his stomach and rests his chin on a jeweled fist. (Rings are his favorite ornament.) His perfect backside shines in the sidereal light, copper-brown. "I've been trying to figure out who. And well, it has to be Danielle, don't you think?"

"Danielle?"

"She just isn't the Hero type, Stir. Haven't you noticed? She's strange. She's not playing to the cameras, she doesn't like multiple sex partners, she's stuck on her brother, and the most damning peculiarity of all, she's smart."

I shake my head. "She's no scientist. She's just disillusioned. With five missions back-to-back, she's tired. And she likes to act smart but it's all a performance. I can see right through her."

Armstrong shrugs. "I don't know. Who else could it be?"

"If it's true," I say, grasping the end of my lavender bleached ponytail and brushing it across my lips, "what would be the point of putting a scientist on *Lacrosse*?"

"To muck it up? Make us look bad?" Armstrong guesses.

I inhale. My hair smells of rain. "Why?"

He rolls to his side. There's a damp imprint of his body on the smooth deck. The starlight tries to absorb it. "I've heard the technicians and scientists want back in space. Maybe if we fail, they can get public support?"

"Hmm." I watch the porthole, the silent, night-woven fields we Heroes love so much. Nothing moves. It's as if we're at a standstill and not hurtling 628 million kilometers in eight weeks to the largest planet in our solar system. I suddenly have the urge to write bad poetry. Armstrong, whose specialty is drama, will later recite it. Stuff like this is what the public craves. It's something our scientists seem incapable of giving. Our fans pay well for videos of our months in space.

And we treat them to every delicacy, from sex to sculpture to daring acrobatic space-walks. Our lives are a performance. Art.

Armstrong suggests, "You should check into the background of everyone on board. As captain, you're the only one with access."

That would be real work, something I'm not used to. The script never calls for a real mystery where the loose ends aren't already figured out and programmed into us. This is supposed to be a straight-forward voyage, filled mainly with sex and traditional psychological tension. Armstrong and I even have a high-charged lover's quarrel prepared for the return trip. But now everything is wrong. With Danielle breaking character and acting smart, the camaraderie is off-balance. And now if the rumor is true, well, I don't want to think about the money I'm going to lose when those royalties don't come. Real life is a bore. No one will buy the recordings of this voyage if we have a real problem to solve.

"Moon crap," I sigh.

*

There is one section of the bridge which isn't just a model. It contains a readout screen, and access to the PTB library computers back on Earth. I program it for reading since I can read twice as fast as it talks, and download each crew member's personnel file. Just that small process gives me a headache. The first one I cue up is Danielle's.

It is less than suspicious. If she's a scientist, then she's been undercover as a Hero for ten years. This is her twenty-second mission – first time under my command – and she likes to read. Because of her beauty, she's a popular crewer, but her love of the classics bores viewers. As with all Heroes, she's bisexual. PTB thought that with her current carnal interest in her twin brother, Drac, she might climb the popularity chart. In one month she's gone from 104 to 44. I

116

make a footnote of my own to log onto the existing vids of her and Drac next time I'm in the playroom. To rise 60 points on the popularity level, she and Drac must be some kind of team to see.

Drac's file follows.

I scroll down to his popularity rating. Usually I don't care about numbers. They don't affect my performance. But when I see Drac's is number two, right below John Luke's and two above me, I do a double-take. I'm thinking, how can anyone get to number two on their first mission after only one month's worth of recordings? The tapes haven't even had time to be properly marketed.

Coincidentally, he chooses that moment to walk onto the bridge.

I turn and my eyes must still be registering shock, because he asks if I'm all right.

"Sure," I sputter. "Just fine."

He looks at the screen just before I deftly flick it off, then walks past me toward the main viewer.

Drac wears black Levis with the seat missing, a mesh gold shirt. His black, old-fashioned cowboy boots click like hammers against the deck.

"Isn't this the middle of your sleep period?" he asks. His shoulder-length hair, black like Danielle's, is haloed by stars.

"It's too hot to sleep," I say, going to my chair in the center of the bridge.

Blocked stars are revealed as he shifts, barely turning. His face is in profile now as he glances out the corner of his eye at me sitting on my captain's altar. He laughs. "You know the temperature never varies. It's impossible for it to be too hot."

"Well, it changes in my head. My skull is throbbing. I've been thinking too much to sleep."

"Take two aspirin and call me in the morning." He can be really funny when he wants to, but that joke is a century old.

When I don't laugh, he comes over and hunkers at my feet. He's a rough-hewn, gangly image of his female twin. His blue eyes are hard, chipped azure. His mouth, when it smiles, doesn't curve. Where Danielle seems sweet, Drac appears dangerous. For a moment I have the queasy feeling he hates me. Then it disappears as his long fingers touch my leather-tucked knee. "How 'bout a bedtime story?"

Sounds great, but unfortunately Armstrong wore me out. "What about Danielle?"

"What about her? She doesn't want you, you know. But she isn't me."

I lean forward and kiss him on the lips. When I pull back I notice he's carefully watching me. Too careful. I press my hand between my eyes and wince. "Headache," I say. "Besides, I'm saving you for a rainy day." The starlight seems to surge as I rise to my feet. He doesn't move. When I try to step past him, Drac reaches out so fast and grabs my ankle that I have no time to respond. He pulls my foot out from under me and I topple backwards to the hard deck, whacking my head on the gilded captain's throne.

"Star-shit! What'd you do that for?" My vision swims. My voice, strained with shock, comes out strangled. He straddles me and grabs both my wrists.

"I don't take rejection well," he says. Then, snarling, "You know, don't you?" His face fills my view. There's a glimmer of moisture on the corner of his mouth. Is this the same Drac I thought I lusted after? "I saw you accessing my file. Who'd you talk to? What's the plan? To dump me at Jupiter? Gas me in my sleep?" His hands drop mine and go for a tight grip on my throat. By this time I'm bucking like a star wrestler, trying to throw him off. I don't think about the royalties for this play. I don't think about the awards. It's life that precious to a Hero. Life first. Then the stars. Then sex.

This guy is definitely not in my category. But a scientist? I never would've guessed.

"Can't breathe," I say, retching, pushing at his wrists.

"What were you going to do to me?" he yells, banging my head against the deck.

He's bigger than me, stronger, but I'm a Hero. Primed for this. I've got twenty-five years experience on him, and a new body. I push hard enough to get him off-balance. His grip loosens and I fling him with all my strength to one side, kicking at his bent legs in the process. I pummel his face with my fists, and thick, red blood flows from his nose. His skull knocks against the captain's chair and that really slows him down.

I grab his shoulders, shake. His dark head lolls. "Until now, it was your sister I suspected, you idiot. And there is no plan!"

"Screw me," he says, and as most folks do after taking a Hero's punch direct in the face, he passes out.

*

I say we grease the rat-fucked son of a bitch!" Armstrong says dramatically, making his bejeweled hand into a fist.

"Oh quit quoting famous classics, Arm. You're boring," Hunter complains. She's lounging on a table, eating dehydrated fudge. Thick brown hair hangs in her face. Her right bare foot rests on Drac's gold-mesh-covered shoulder. The shirt is stained brown from the nosebleed I gave him.

At the table, facing away from Hunter and toward the rest of us, Drac Blacque sits tied to a chair. A blue silk scarf gags him. Every time Hunter's toes tickle his cheek, he rolls his eyes, very Danielle-like.

Danielle, in the far corner, watches, cheeks tear-streaked. So far, she's said nothing.

119

"We're not going to 'grease' anyone," I say, watching my captive's reaction. His nose shows signs of a mottled, purple bruise. His eyes are the same hard blue. Up to now, he's revealed no emotion.

"Why not?" Sigourney Quinn, dancer, asks. "He attacked the captain. That's a capital offense."

"Yeah," Shariff Parque, *Lacrosse's* vague excuse for a doctor – those he's more talented at spacewalking – adds. "He tried to kill you."

I watch the chiseled blue eyes. For a moment I think I see fear spark them. "Maybe he was afraid for his life," I say.

"What?" Hunter's chocolate-smeared lips scowl.

"Maybe he thought I knew about him and was going to kill him." Now Drac watches me with a new interest. His dark brows rise slightly.

Darcy Chance, dressed all in black and the best singer on board, says quietly, "He's entitled to a fair trial."

Now Danielle steps forward. Despite the tears, her voice is strong. "How can it be fair? He's entitled to a jury of his peers and there's none on this ship. We're all Heroes."

Everyone turns and stares at her. "Are you a Hero? Really?" Sigourney asks. Her black eyes glower.

"I didn't know about Drac! All my family are Heroes. But now, now that we know the truth, that he's a scientist," he spits the words, "that's no reason to...to...kill him!"

I can't help but feel sorry for her. After all, I still want her. If it weren't for her true devotion to her brother, I know I would've had her by now. Besides, she's wearing that red lace get-up again. I can't not believe her.

"She's telling the truth," I say.

"She's arguing to spare his life," Armstrong says, nodding.

"Life. A Hero's first priority," Shariff says.

The others reluctantly agree.

"She's one of us," I say. I hold my hand out to her. She comes to my side and grasps it.

"Well." I glance down at her. "What do you suggest we do?"

Danielle looks up at me, blinks away tears and says, "Let him speak." She turns toward her brother. "He'll tell me the truth."

"He didn't before," Armstrong mutters under his breath.

"Do it." I nod at Hunter. She puts down her fudge and scoots across the table on her ass. Her hands undo the silk scarf and free his mouth. She uses it to tie up her heavy hair, then goes back to her fudge.

Drac coughs, licks his lips.

"What were you going to do, Drac?" Danielle asks softly.

He looks away.

"Drac?"

Their eyes meet, blue on blue. "You wouldn't understand."

"Try us," I say.

Drac lets out a forced sigh. "Do you realize that for 80 years space travel has been stagnant? Nothing's changed. Oh, you bring back samples, but any computer could do that. You do Hollywood stunts like spacewalking and spacefucking, but what does that teach us? No one byte of information we couldn't get on our own. You're not Heroes. You don't take risks. You don't break new ground. You follow a script. Well, we're tired of it."

"Who's tired of it? You mean scientists?" I ask.

"Yes, damn your ass. With this mission, we wanted to prove that scientists can be just as interesting, just as 'fun'. I was the last person you suspected, wasn't I? Number two on the charts."

Everyone nods dumbly.

"So what were you going to do to this mission?" Darcy asks.

He scowls. "The ship's computers were going to malfunction, endanger the lives of us all. I would be the only one with the knowledge to save us."

"That's impossible," I say. "The computers are controlled from Earth. If there's a malfunction, they fix it."

"I was to set it up so we'd plummet into Jupiter, into all that hydrogen and heavy gravity. The computers were to take more time to fix than we had. We'd break apart before control could be regained. So I was to take them off-line and pilot us out."

I frown because, you see, this is my ship and even I don't know how to fly her. "You know how to pilot this thing?"

"Yeah." Drac studies his lap.

"Wow," Armstrong says.

"What kind of scientist are you?" I ask.

"Astrophysicist. Specialties…" He looks up. "The nature of stars and long-term spaceflight simulation."

"How come you never told me you were a scientist?" Danielle steps forward, bent to his level on the deck, glaring. "I'm your best friend."

"You became a Hero right out of school. You were never home. I never told you I went to school for eight years after that because you wouldn't understand. Heroes are well-known for their prejudice toward scientists. So I never told you where I worked while you were gone in space. And, the typical self-centered Hero, you never asked."

"I thought you were a bum." Danielle reaches out to touch his cheek.

Drac turns away.

I feel that strange queasiness in my stomach again when I look at him. He really hates us.

The rest of my crew shifts uncomfortably. There's a brief silence.

"So, what are we going to do with him?" Armstrong scratches his left buttock and stares around the room.

"Let him go," I say.

Five gasps fill the air. Only Danielle, Drac and I are silent.

"You can't let him go ahead with his plan," Hunter insists.

"He tried to kill you," Shariff says, crossing his arms.

"I thought he would kill *me*. I was trying to get the truth out of him!" Drac explains.

"Would you have killed me?" I ask.

"Would you have killed me if you'd known my plan?"

"Heroes don't kill except in self-defense."

"I *was* defending myself," Drac says glancing at us all in turn. "When I saw you on the bridge with my file up, I thought you knew about me. I thought all of you knew." He looks longest at Danielle.

Danielle kneels at his feet and touches his bound hands. "And you think you're so smart," she whispers, kissing his folded fingers.

*

Space seems a lot blacker, the bulkheads a duller gray, when one of your crew is unhappy.

We voted 5-2 to let Drac go. He seemed harmless enough, since I alerted our Earth-based computer techs to search for anomalous programs in our systems.

We all watched Drac slink off in those seatless pants of his, go to his room and immediately switch on the privacy light.

No one's seen him since.

As a result, everyone's spirits decline. Hunter loses her appetite for fudge. Armstrong loses his for sex, and I feel guilty to have stolen the stars from someone who, in his own tedious way, might be as deserving as I.

This is a real life problem, and as captain I'm obligated to solve it. I'm not liking it one bit. Problems are always best handled when you know the outcome beforehand.

I consider paying Drac a personal visit, but I can't think of what we'd talk about now that I know we have nothing in common. Still, we have three months of our mission left and it will surely be a video disaster if I can't get him to participate again in Hero activities.

Since it's my responsibility to fix things, I decide I must learn everything about Drac to better understand the nature of his 'being'. I've never known a scientist before.

My first step is to call up vids of him in action: joking with the crew, eating (he's a vegetarian), staring at the stars and trying to paint them (he's terrible with color), running games in the playroom (he likes group interactive sports), having sex (now I see why he's number two on the chart.) At first I see nothing that sets him apart from other Heroes; in fact, he's got major Personality Charisma Factor, which is what the PTBs look for when signing us up. After awhile of viewing his life habits, however, I notice an inquisitiveness in him that is not present in the others, including Danielle. Danielle is smart, but it's all book-learned. Drac figures things out, and he has a kind of curiosity that shows up at the oddest moments. In one scene I watch him inspect a doorframe, running his hands along the sloped angles. In another, he's got his ear cocked to the wall of the main engine unit, listening to who knows what. I've never heard a sound from our engines. Also, I watch him beat my live-mystery game in less than an hour.

My eyes burning, my brain filled to busting with Drac Drac Drac recordings, I invite Danielle to my quarters for dinner. Because I know she will decline, I make it an order.

She stalks into my room wearing layers of black silk draped across her breasts, and long pieces of silk tied at the hip, leaving her midriff and right thigh bare. One piece she has used as a scarf to hide her hair.

"Why are you making me do this?" she grumbles as she goes to sit at the temporary table in the center of the room. She faces my port window to the stars.

"I want to talk about your brother."

"Please. I've been humiliated enough."

"I know. I'm sorry. But I have to know a few things. You know him best. He's your twin."

"But I don't want to talk about him," she says quietly. "I'm ashamed. And I feel betrayed."

"Were you really fooled by him?"

She nods, plays with a thick gold bracelet o her forearm. It is the color of candlelight.

"Danielle, he's got great PCF, which might throw anyone off, but you had to notice certain things about him. His curiosity, for one."

"Yes." She shrugs, fingers the silverware.

I pour us each a glass of dehydrated-just-add-water white wine. She takes a slow sip before continuing. Her upper lip glistens. "I thought he outgrew it. He always experimented with things when we were kids. He made stuff like, you know, rocketships and bombs. Once he set the house on fire with some kind of anti-gravity device he was trying to invent. It was just kid stuff, though, just a phase. He was so likeable, funny, you know, born to perform, that the rest of us just thought he was a natural-made Hero. Then he disappeared for awhile. He told me he was traveling the world. He wanted to see it all before he got older.

"But he was lying."

"His whole life is a lie."

"Would you have accepted him if he told you the truth?"

Danielle looks up, blue eyes motionless in her star-lit face. "Yes."

"Is that the truth?"

She looks down. "I love him. I would have accepted it. Eventually."

125

I turn toward the spacescape, sipping my wine. "We set ourselves up as superior."

"It's our job," she says.

"Yes, it's expected. We are, after all, Heroes. But sometimes I wonder who the real heroes are, with a small 'h'."

"People who brave the unknown, or do the impossible," she replies.

"And we don't really do that, do we?"

"No," she agrees. "I've come to realize that over the years. But we still serve a purpose. We keep the industry going. We fund it. We make it fun and entertaining so people invest."

"That's the way it's always been, throughout history. You need flashy people or hype to sell things, even if those things are necessary, good for you, for the benefit of all Mankind. The real heroes never get the credit."

Danielle leans her chin on her upturned palm. Her eyes seek the view behind me and barely succeed in holding back a wave of shimmering tears. "How Drac must hate us."

*

Despite the fact that Drac is not confined to his quarters, he doesn't come out for two days, not even for food.

Much as I don't know what to say to him, I feel obligated, as captain, to schedule a visit.

The dinner with Danielle has given me some insight, but I'm still frustrated by my failure to seduce her. Facing Drac in my current mood is a disturbing prospect, and yet it seems he's starving himself in there, or performing some such dramatic gesture.

I'm just about to the point of convincing myself to let him starve and call it a night, when Hunter bustles into the mess, her thick hair obscuring most of her face. The silver suit she wears clings so tightly from ankle to throat, I wonder if her circulation is impaired.

126

"There you are," she announces to the room.

"I've been here for quite awhile," I point out. "What is it?"

"Sig's been tapping into Earth a lot, following the charts. We thought you might want to know what we've just found."

"What?" Real dramatic tension is so different from pretend. Despite the pills Shariff gave me, my headache has returned.

"Drac's just gone to number one."

My mouth opens and freezes that way. I imagine I must look like a six-foot fish in pain.

"Not only that, it bumped John Luke to third."

Regaining my voice, I ask, "Well, then, who's second now?"

"You."

"Me?"

"It's upset the whole male listing. Apparently, someone got hold of the interrogation tape and before the PTB could formally issue it, pirate copies got out. The civs love him. They love that he's a scientist." Her lips curl in a display of disgust. "They love that you stuck up for him."

"Great."

"I know. It's terrible, isn't it? The bastard has nice form in *danse l'amour*, a perfect PCF rating, and he's smart to boot! He didn't even need to save the ship to get votes." She harrumphs dejectedly and hops upon a nearby table, lying back. "He's ruining the competition."

The mess has the largest porthole, rectangular and running the length of the room. From the angle of our ship, you can see Sol becoming more distant every day. Right now she's the size of an apricot, and all that golden light pulsing at us makes Hunter, sheathed in silver, glow.

I get up and slowly approach her. "Ruining the competition?" I say. "No. It just spices it up."

She watches me hungrily. "Then let's compete." Already her hand has found the invisible seams of her suit. The pieces of it fall away from her like water, her voluptuous skin awash with stars. Her breasts are warm and flowing against my palms.

My leather comes off with less grace, but neither of us cares. It's one of the best performances of my life. My only regret is that no one bursts in on the scene for a meal. They miss the privilege of seeing, live, what I'm sure will be a classic tape once released. But no recording could come close to expressing the power of the real thing.

Afterwards, I find that my headache is gone.

*

In my hand is a plate with the heat turned up. Its contents include samplings of my favorite vegetarian delicacies: corn pasta, artichoke salad, seaweed mousse.

Sigourney comes around a corner and raises both her dyed-white eyebrows. "You should let him rot," she mutters, then moves past me in a scent of orchids.

I turn toward the door. First I knock. I expect no answer and have the override ready just in case, but after a mere two seconds the door opens.

Drac's blue eyes move from the plate in my hands to my face. "Well," he says, stepping away from the door to let me in. "You're the first."

He doesn't look like hell, but he's got a tired slump. His face is pale, gaunt. Hew wears an ugly pair of shorts, red, which are baggy and show off nothing of his finer qualities. I see an old bag of dried banana chips on his bunk. It's empty.

"Been living on that?" I ask, nodding toward the bag.

He doesn't answer. He stands, arms folded, facing the stars. Amid a disarray of pillows, game headbands, boots, backless jeans and what look like real computer notebooks, I find a clear spot on the deck and set down the plate.

He doesn't move. "Say what you came to say."

"Well," I begin. "I would, but I don't know *what* to say. I've never talked to a scientist before."

"Idiot," he mutters under his breath.

"What is your plan now? To just disappear from this mission? Lock yourself away for the next three months?"

He doesn't answer.

I go to his bunk, sweep aside strewn pillows and clothing, and take a seat.

"The stars look pretty tonight, don't they?" I venture. Actually, they always look pretty much the same.

His head bows; his arms unfold. I can see his fists clench. "We sleep the beauty of the night away, the dark wonder, secrets kept secret."

"What?"

He turns, grimacing. "Don't you recognize it? It's a poem *you* wrote."

"Oh. Yeah."

"I thought you were writing about not being inquisitive, observant, aware. But you don't even remember writing it, do you?" Beneath a tangle of dark hair, his blue eyes glare.

"I've got tomes of that star-crap."

"I hate you," he says suddenly.

"Okay," I reply. "Now that we've got that out in the open…"

"You don't even try, do you? You don't even care."

My hands rise, palms-up in question. "About what?"

"About why things are the way they are, what makes them work." He takes a step toward me. The stars grip his shoulders.

"You mean science?"

He nods.

"I failed physics I school. Got a D in eleventh grade biology. I managed to skip chemistry altogether. Why would I pursue something I can't possibly understand?"

"Why pursue Danielle," he asks.

I stare at him. He's not trying to be funny, but I don't make the connection. Finally, I answer. "Because I love to fuck."

"Exactly."

I sigh loudly. "I don't get it."

"You love life. You love the stars. But what do you really know about either one?" He's starting to get interested. I can tell by the stance of his body. And his eyes are more alert.

I'm beginning to get perturbed. "I'm not an intellectual like you."

"Says who?" He comes to stand in front of me.

"I'm no good at figuring things out. I saw you run that mystery tape in less than an hour. I haven't gotten through it yet."

"I used to play it all the time in college. It took me a year to figure it out."

"Oh."

He waves my comment aside. "But that's not the point. Why does the PTB stress that knowledge is boring, that figuring out answers to real questions is low entertainment?"

"It doesn't rate well, that's a fact. And these missions cost money. They have to pay for themselves."

"They don't make scientific exploration *exciting* enough. There're fewer and fewer scientists because the media say it's drudgery to be one. And so nothing new is being done in space."

"Well, there you're wrong. This mission is a first. We're going to see if Jupiter has a core and what it's really made of. It might even make us all rich if we find diamonds or something."

He shakes his head, laughs. "Not diamonds. More like iron. Or gold. This mission isn't for furthering knowledge. It's a mining job."

"It's still worth our while," I argue. "Gold, you say?"

He rolls his eyes, very Danielle-like.

"Well, how do you expect me to react?" I ask. "This is the biggest planet in the solar system. If it's a gold mine..."

"Well, at least you know that much," he grumbles.

I pat the bunk next to me. "Sit down, Drac." To my surprise, he does. I stiffen a little, not sued to being in such close proximity to a scientist, but it gets easier with each passing minute. He's acting pretty Hero-ic, so it's easy to dismiss what he really is. And he smells good. Like spice.

"I was working on long-distance spaceflight. For trips outside the solar system."

"Really?" So hit me: it does sound intriguing.

"Yeah." After awhile, he hangs his head. The fringe of his long hair shadows his chest. "But that's not good enough. It seems nothing real is good enough for publicity unless it's sanctioned by the PTB."

"Well, that's not entirely true. We got distracted when I first came in here. There is something I want to tell you. Something you should know."

"What?" He sounds bored.

"It seems reality can be 'good enough' as you put it. You're number one on the popularity charts, and you didn't land there until after it was discovered you were really a scientist."

His head comes up. His mouth is a perfect, dark 'O'. "Huh? Eh?" It's as if there's a light temporarily out in his eyes. They look clouded, dazed.

"You even beat me out: I'm number two."

The light goes on. Blue depths sparkle. He leans toward me. "Really?"

"And you didn't even have to save us all from dying to get there."

"Really?" He grabs my shoulders, shakes me. "Really?"

"Yes." I try to shrug out of his grip but he's too strong. Instead, I just laugh.

"Really? I'm number one? Right now?"

"Yes. Yes!"

He pulls me to him, kisses me hard on the forehead, then jumps up and starts dancing and hopping around the room like a deranged psychotic. "I'm number one," he says to himself, repeating it over and over. It becomes a song. "I'm number one."

"You're rating is going to fall rapidly if you don't stop that soon," I yell.

He turns. His grin is all I need to see to make me realize my words are lies.

Drac doesn't need to *do* anything. No daring rescue attempts, no circus spacewalks, no bad art, no acting, he just exudes natural Hero-ism. He's what the PTB has been looking for for decades without ever knowing it.

Hunter is right. The competition will never be the same. PCF, brains, looks, sexual prowess, he's got it all. None of us Heroes are a match. And, I fear, by the end of this scene our world as we know it will never be the same.

*

We're on the bridge, staring outward through the wall window screen. The stars are eyes, little bursts of wisdom, of beauty. We are but shadows in their bloom.

"How can you love those lights in the sky and not yearn to know what they're called, how they speak, what they're made of?" He leans back in the captain's gold chair and his eyes flash with the intimacy of knowledge and wonder. I'm ready for it now, ready for words and numbers and tongue-tangling theories I've got the right teacher. And I've got time. Besides, the projected returns on this tape promise to beat out all the past top vid hits combined."

"All right, Drac," I say, watching the ancient light play in his black hair. I lean against the armrest, the closest I'll get anymore to my chair until I've earned it. The first step is always the hardest. "Teach me." I stare at where the gold

132

mesh breaks away to reveal the taut muscles of his chest. Then, with an effort, I glance up and out to the undying universe. "Begin with the texture of stars."

A New Design

when they made the starships
to look like swans
I realized
a poet had designed them
They took flight
over ponds of snowmoons
and meteors clung
to the edge of the sky
such beauty
such silken vessels
the sparkling distance
to devour

Afterword

The above stories and poems span some 20 years of writing and are a sampling of the many, many tales I have told throughout the years. Several of these stories were written in the late 1990s. Others in 2012-2014. Half have been previously published, half are brand new.

It's hard for me to categorize my works. I have published in all genres, but when I sit down to write I don't think of genre, I just write what I love in the moment. I simply get an idea/character and the compulsion to write comes over me. I have always enjoyed the ghostly, odder edges of reality. And I love looking toward distant futures. My influences come from just about everywhere.

I thank you for reading my stories and poems.

If you have time, please think about reviewing this book on Amazon.

For more information about my books, visit my author page on Amazon.

Visit my blog at: http://wendyrathbone.blogspot.com/

My best to all the readers,

Wendy Rathbone
author of: *Letters to an Android, Pale Zenith,* and more.

Credits

The Dream in a Box was previously published in the anthology *Mutation Nation.*

The Thin Place was previously published in the anthology *Amaranth.*

The Texture of Stars was previously published in the anthology *Air Fish.*

The Beautiful People was previously published in the anthology *Bending the Landscape - Science Fiction.*

Under the World was previously published in *2001: A Poetry Anthology,* and nominated for a Rhysling Award. It also appeared in the author's collection, *Dancing in the Haunted Woodlands,* winner of Yellow Bat Press's 2003 chapbook contest, and is currently in print in the author's omnibus collection containing seven of her out of print poetry books, *Unearthly.*

Sons of Neverland was written as a tribute to the novel *Sons of Neverland* by Della Van Hise.

Letters to an Android

by

Wendy Rathbone

(warning: this novel contains starboats, spacesickness, poisonous green skies, emotional androids and haiku)

Part One

1. Liyan

Liyan had just finished repairs on a coupling unit in the spaceport's huge workshop. A job well done. He threw off his work gloves for the last time and did not look back.

He went outside to breathe the ion-laced air of the tarmac, and looked up at the dark green, force-field encased sky and the space tunnel where a line of hovering round-ships waited for orders to set down. Laser repair lights winked scarlet on the landing field. A rare rocket stretched its white fume into the emerald atmosphere. It would create its own tunnel to escape the force-field without an atmospheric breach. What they were testing with it he had no idea. Nor did he care. This was his last day of work here.

Earlier in the week he'd gotten his flight posting. The one he'd dreamed of and worked toward, attending school 25 hours a week as well as holding down a first level mechanic's job.

At age 20, he would be entering the world of C&C Starlines at full ensign ranking. He'd gotten the go-ahead seven days ago. Barely enough time to give notice to his landlord and pack his small room and the few personal items he wanted to take with him.

Adrenalin rushed through him. He gasped a deep breath of the ashy air and realized he was grinning. A co-worker clanked by him in a black-scarred, bulky silver protective suit. The helmet made a square silhouette against the backdrop of the river-hued sky. Evan looked like some old fashioned robot from the cover of an ancient Earth magazine about aliens and metal men. Evan said, voice muffled from the helmet, "We're gonna miss you around here."

Liyan wasn't going to miss any of this. But he said, "Thanks. Me, too."

"Come by the Aurora later." He sounded like he was speaking around a wad of tissue from an echo chamber. "We're all going to Rory's. We'll buy your drinks."

The Grand Aurora was the port's only five-star hotel with the biggest and most popular bar called Rory's Bar.

Liyan said, "I'm staying there until tomorrow when we get shuttled to the starport. My apartment's already rented to someone else."

"Good, then we'll see you at Rory's!" Evan clomped across the threshold and disappeared inside the workshop.

*

Even the cheapest room at the Aurora dripped luxury. Silk and damask. Real oak furniture. Satin comforters and tapestried walls.

For a few minutes, Liyan rolled on the bed in soft euphoria. A crystal chandelier sang its refracted violetpinkgold essence into his brain. He smelled a fine mist on the air, something like spice and fresh grass and a kind of creamy soap used only in bubble baths. He actually intended to have one of those. But later.

Now, he got up and changed into more trendy clothing: a furnace blue button up shirt and black trousers with low-heeled, newly polished work boots. He would have a uniform at his new job, but tonight he could still choose his own colors. He combed his smooth brown hair which was a bit long to the shoulders now. He figured C&C would take care of any hair style they required from him, so he hadn't rushed for a haircut.

When he felt presentable enough, he grabbed his key and moneycard and headed for the bar.

His friends greeted him with high enthusiasm. Liyan smiled until his cheeks ached.

Beer. Whiskey. Expensive wine. His friends offered him anything he wanted. Such good men and women. They had been fine co-workers, but he hadn't gotten close to any of them. His schooling and his dreaming got in the way of any social life. But they were still generous and they all clapped him on the back as if he were some hero going off to save the universe.

In fact, he was going further than most of them ever hoped to get in a lifetime.

The bar-light was warm and gold. The drinks weren't as watered as usual and packed a punch.

Not wanting to be hung-over on the shuttle ride the next day, Liyan slowed his drinking pace. He wandered away from the crowd toward the shadows by the end of the long, curving counter, and asked the young man making tall, fizzing concoctions of something purple and glittery for a glass of water.

The man turned, slim and graceful, hair the hue of Technicolor seas on old 'wave' programs about true-Earth when it still supported life. He had to have been supremely distracted not to have noticed this man until now. His face had such a fine-tuned edge to it, angled and curved in just the right places, the eyes wide and down-turned enough to be coy but still masculine. Even more shocking, perhaps: the irises were the same shade as the violet fizzing drinks he'd been preparing.

The man placed a glass of ice water in front of him. Liyan hadn't meant to stare, but the man didn't appear to mind. The bartender asked, voice a low tremor on the air, "Is the celebration going on over there for you?"

"I'm leaving tomorrow, a job on a ship with C&C Starlines."

"I see. New realms. New experiences. A new life."

"That's about right."

"Then I, too, would like to wish you all fortune in your travels."

Liyan blinked, oddly pleased though this man was a stranger. "Thank you."

"Where to, first, if I may ask?"

Before Liyan could answer, a waiter came to pick up the three purple drinks. Soon they were alone again. Liyan had completely forgotten his friends. He said, "When the crew is settled and the ship readied, I'm told the first destination is Fair-Orb."

He nodded, his eyes going from mauve to gray in his neat attention. "That far. You'll be a true star-man, then."

"Technically, yes. I passed the tests in the top fifth percentile in nav. I'll be going on the long-hauls." Most people didn't pass them at all, not their first time or their tenth.

"Impressive," the bartender said.

"For as long as I can remember I've wanted this. It's been all work and no play for me." He sighed, finally remembering his friends, looking over his shoulder. They hadn't missed him yet. They were all occupied with their drinks and their jokes.

"They say on Fair-Orb the stars meet the sea," the bartender said.

140

Liyan raised his eyebrows at such a beautiful but true statement. "It is made of mostly water."

"And at night the towers that jut out of the sea look suspended in space. You truly cannot tell where the seas end and the stars begin. Alas, I will never see it."

Liyan lifted his glass and took a sip of the cold, plain water. It cooled him, but the heat of excitement did not wane. He set the glass down and held out his hand. "My name is Liyan."

The man raised his hand to meet his palm to palm. "Cobalt. I am at your service."

"At my…?" It was a confusing line, one Liyan had not heard before.

"Perhaps I should explain. I will never see Fair-Orb in my lifetime. I am locked into my work contract here. Forever."

"Work contract?" Liyan frowned. "Oh. I didn't realize…you're an android?"

"It is a compliment that it was not obvious to you."

"I thought you were a really pretty…human." He chuckled. "That's all."

"Thank you," the android said. "Of course now that you know this fact about me, you know I have no rights. Despite the longing in my thoughts." His full, pink lips curved into a tiny smile. "I can only travel in other people's stories. And I travel in my dreams."

Liyan did know that androids had no human rights. But he knew little else. "You dream?"

"Of course. All beings dream."

Liyan said, "I've always been taught that androids are machines and that it's wrong to think they aren't. But I know you have organic components."

"Yes, all my components are organic."

"So you're just like…like a person."

"I am."

"It's sad, then."

"What is?"

"That you can't leave." Liyan looked at the purple eyes and blue hair of his bartender. The skin of the face was such a perfect, smooth bronze. He should've guessed. But he'd never met anyone like him before. All he knew was that androids were bought and owned by the extremely wealthy who were the only ones who could afford them. So why was this one working at the Grand Aurora? "The hotel bought you to tend bar?"

"I do whatever is required. All jobs here. The owner inherited me five years ago."

"Oh." Liyan watched as a drink order came in and Cobalt began preparing it. The android had not dismissed him, so he waited. It seemed such a waste, someone with the capacity of Cobalt in mind and body mixing beverages in a hotel bar. Android brains were grown for obedience and brilliance. He would've passed the C&C company tests in the first percentile.

When Cobalt turned his attention back to him, Liyan said, "I have an idea."

Cobalt shifted his head in question.

"Maybe you can't leave here, but I could write you on the wave. Tell you firsthand of my adventures."

The android managed to look authentically wistful. "I would like that."

"You're thinking maybe I'll forget as soon as I leave here, but I won't. I will write to you. I promise."

Cobalt said, "I'll be waiting to hear from you, then."

Liyan watched the long, perfect fingers of the android drum the countertop as if in human anticipation.

"Do I wave you here at the hotel?"

"Yes. My name is my address on the hotel's system."

"Cobalt," Liyan said. "I won't forget it."

*

2. Cobalt

Cobalt waited two weeks and heard nothing from Liyan. He did not expect any correspondence, but he had hoped for it. Just a little. As much as he allowed himself any hope in his life of menial servitude.

Sometimes he looked toward the green-storm harbors of the shipyards, watching the agate skies roil and roll in the vapors the ships left in their wakes and he would recall his conversation with Liyan verbatim. He would remember the young man's hands, how they trembled against the water glass in excitement and maybe even a little anxiety. He would remember the exact shade of his hair, autumn-leaf brown, and how deep that youthful, brown-eyed stare.

It made him content to know Liyan was out there somewhere beyond the port, moving into the enchanting embrace of other worlds and beyond, into the darkrush of driftless void.

He really didn't expect Liyan to ever keep his promise. But if he did, Cobalt wondered what he would do if he received a wave. Should he respond? What did he have to say, to give? His life consisted of work. He wanted beauty, too, but he had never really found it. Was there any point in describing the fine suits he wore when he was concierge, or how deftly less-than-gentle men took them off him when they rented him from his owner for a night?

And what about his owner? An old man who couldn't care less about him except that he earned. Cobalt did everything he was told. A letter attesting to that seemed, to him, a very boring one indeed.

Sometimes, when he tried to see the stars through the oily gaseous skies of the port, he actually hoped Liyan would not write, that he would stay away and never look back. Just go. Go.

It was what he wanted to do himself. He could only imagine it. But now he had a face to put to his imaginings. He could live vicariously through Liyan.

*

One particularly unfortunate and annoying night, as Cobalt bathed in a lilac-scented tub and attended to handprint-shaped bruising on his thighs, he heard his wavescreen chirp.

His wavescreen only did that when his owner wanted him for a job. But he'd done his job for the evening. He'd been given the rest of the night off to repair and sleep.

What, then, could this be?

Slowly, he rose from the tub. He dripped onto the bathroom rug, delicately drying his sensitive skin, then put on a robe and went to see what it was.

The amber light blinked: *Message. Message.*

He lit the screen and read the odd address. Unfamiliar. His heart twitched in his chest.

He reached out, hesitant at first, and touched the address.

The message appeared.

Dear Cobalt:

I have not forgotten you. Not for one moment. I even hope you might have missed me. I don't mean to be cruel in saying that, only hopeful because we have only met once and I think I am presuming far too much. I may have passed C&C requirements at the top of my class, but I'm still a bit remedial in social interaction. But I made a promise to you. And I want to keep it.

Also, you made an impression on me. I can't forget your face. I think I miss you more than the friends I worked with for two years. Isn't that strange?

And now I want to erase that last paragraph. But I won't. I am very young compared to a lot of my ship-mates, so I think you should allow me to be a bit dumb.

I want to tell you where I am. And I want to make it good for you. You might be able to see a picture on the wave, but it's still not the same as being here.

The starport for the liner, and other stop-over ships, is a giant cube with fifty floors. Inside that cube everything is uniform, the rooms and offices square and all the same. It isn't much to speak of. But looking at the port from outside is like looking at a black metal square window floating against the immortal dark. It's a blank, dark page in space waiting for words. And there are starships in the margins. They hang there as if doodled by some insane, giant hand.

In every distance are tiny swarms of stars.
I hope these words help you see what I see.
The starliner is almost ready. I am well.

Your friend,

Liyan

Cobalt let the milky light of the wave bathe his face as he read it a second time. And a third.

This was a first for him. Never before had he received a wave from anyone who did not want something from him, but only wanted to give.

He touched 'reply' though he had no idea what to say in return. He began slowly.

Dear Liyan:

From my room in the Grand Aurora I sit and read your words. They give me a unique vision that I greatly welcome. I will take that vision with me to my work.

Now when I look at the green-marbled skies of this port I will not be as sad.

And I will keep seeing your starships in the margins.
You fulfilled your promise to me. I thank you.

Your friend,

Cobalt

He brushed the 'send' light with the tip of his forefinger.

When he went to bed, he'd forgotten all about his pain.

*

The next night he saw another wave message light flashing in his room.

Dear Cobalt:

We leave tomorrow. While in foldspace there will be no waves. Navigation in this instance is always unpredictable. It could be days or weeks before I can respond.

In the meantime, I wanted to say I had no idea you were sad. But of course this is my oversight. You are trapped at the Grand Aurora for your lifespan which, in the research I have done on androids since I met you, appears to be quite long. The unpleasantness of your situation affects me. I wish I could do something to help. Instead, I will write you when I can. I will tell you of my journeys. That I can do.

I am packed and ready to leave. My uniform is stark white trimmed with black ribbing. There is an optional hat, like a flat cap. I refuse to wear it. My boots are black. The C&C logo is embossed on their sides, the Pegasus image a silver brand we wear there and on the cuffs of our shirts.

I will be working in navigation but not up front. I'll work in the chart rooms at the center of the ship. The computers do the math until the charts look like intricate designs of castles, or pyramid piles of leaves, or the bone structures of indescribable monsters. Equation sets are often differentiated by color. The chart rooms resemble galleries of modern art made of tiny numbers.

I fall asleep dreaming of those numbers.

Please write back. Speak of any subject. If I don't receive the wave tomorrow, it will be waiting for me when we get to Fair-Orb.

Your friend,

Liyan.

Again, Cobalt read the message three times, just as he had with the last one. He memorized every word.

He opened a fresh page.

Dear Liyan:

I don't know how to tell you that I long to see indescribable monsters on navigation charts. It is strange to write that. But it is the truth.

If possible, I would next like to hear your experience in foldspace. I have heard it said that no two experiences are alike. Some say time moves slower or faster. Some say inanimate objects appear to shrink or grow before your eyes. Some suffer a kind of spacesickness for the duration and must remain in sleep mode. As you well know, out of foldspace have come revelatory scientific theories, award winning novels, master symphonies, among other amazing human feats of genius.

Do share whatever revelation you may receive, even if it's only one word.

I continue in my duties. There are many I can enjoy and many I cannot enjoy. This is not a complaint, simply a fact. The sadness in me comes, I believe, from the implanted childhood memories that are unreal. Because they did not, in fact, happen, I often wish I did not have them. The theory is they create personality because we are born 'adult'. I can say perhaps they do that, but they cause more pain than pleasure because of developing tastes, likes and dislikes, judgment and subjectivity. If one is going to create a tool, it is cruel to give it emotion, do you not think?

The tediousness of my words appalls me but I leave them.

I look forward to your next wave.

Your friend,

Cobalt

Two weeks passed. In that time he did accounting, reservations, and more bartending. He was also forced to make his body available to two male clients who were selfish and unfriendly. But unlike the last client, they did not leave bruises.

Every night he looked for a message light. None appeared.

He dreamed of watercolor starcharts. He wanted to dream of Liyan. It simply did not happen.

He thought of him often, though, in his white uniform standing on the polished decks of a behemoth ship that cruised the ancient star-lanes. In the image he conjured, Liyan's leaf-hair fell against his brown eyes as he read the math of the stars.

*

ABOUT THE AUTHOR...

Wendy Rathbone has had dozens of stories published in anthologies such as: Hot Blood, Writers of the Future (second place,) Bending the Landscape, Mutation Nation, A Darke Phantastique, and more. Over 500 of her poems have been published in various anthologies and magazines. She won first place in the Anamnesis Press poetry chapbook contest with her book "Scrying the River Styx." Her poems have been nominated for the Science Fiction Poetry Association's Rhysling award at least a dozen times.

Her recent books include:

"Pale Zenith," science fiction novel

"The Foundling," male/male romance novel

"None Can Hold the Dark," sequel to "The Foundling"

"The Secret Sharer," science fiction romance novella

"Unearthly," omnibus collection of 7 out-of-print poetry booklets

"The Vampire Diaries: The Myth," available from Kindle Worlds

"The Vampire Dairies: Deep In the Virginia Woods," available from Kindle Worlds

"My House Is Full of Whispers," erotica short story collection

"Letters To An Android," science fiction novel

"Turn Left at November" poetry collection

"Beneath the Blue Dusk and the Sea" fantasy and science fiction short story collection

She lives in Yucca Valley, CA with her partner of 34 years, Della Van Hise.

LETTERS TO AN ANDROID
Wendy Rathbone

Cobalt is a created human, vat grown and born adult, with no human rights and indentured to serve others for the duration of his life. Liyan is a young man with wanderlust in his eyes, embarking on a career that takes him to the furthest regions of space. The two become unlikely friends and create a memorable long-distance correspondence. Through Liyan, Cobalt gets to explore the universe, living vicariously through his friend's wave transmissions. A strong bond develops between them that not even the stars can put asunder.

Now you know an android who writes poetry.

This is all your fault. Did you not read my last wave telling you extracurricular activities for my kind are discouraged? Of course this is harmless and strangely enjoyable and does not necessarily require me to leave the hotel. Pel would not care if I wrote lines of equations or nonsensical juxtaposed words. As long as the act does not bring my mental state into question.

However, in history, poetry is often written by the rebels.

So we can keep this to ourselves.

Let me know about your lieutenant's test.

And to give you peace of mind, I never believed you observed me as anything other than human.

Some people are and always will be hateful bigots. Most people are simply uncomfortable in speaking to "property." And anyway, friendship, like poetry, is also discouraged.

Your friend,

Cobalt

From the author: www.eyescry.com/html/publications.htm
On Amazon:
http://www.amazon.com/Letters-Android-Wendy-Rathbone-ebook/dp/B00LNE7BMM/

PALE ZENITH
Wendy Rathbone
A Science Fiction Novel

On a far-flung "Earth" in a parallel universe, two factions are fighting a decades-long psychic war. Young talented psychics are being temporarily kidnapped from present day Earth, seemingly at random, to serve as part of one side's psychic army. They are put under the control of spychiatrists, mysterious machines with many limbs that have a programmed ability to travel time and space and universes to kidnap and control carefully selected humans. The humans never know they are being used; when their missions are completed they are brought back to their universe through time and placed back in their beds, their memories wiped.

———————

The shadows wound the tall corridor in muted gold, varnished brown. It seemed as though they were in the bowels of a giant serpent coiled outside time, outside space.

When they left the palace, a familiar sun flourished in a clear, blue sky. But this wasn't their sun. Not Zack's sun. It was an alien star burning within a different galaxy in an all too distant universe. Zack looked up squinting, trying to see if he could peer beyond the sky, beyond the pale of midday and into his own timespace, but there was nothing. Only sunlight. Only the thin atmosphere of an Earth not his own.

His back knotted again. Leo's presence was a gelid space inside his chest, empty. Always before he'd felt a warmth there, a sort of pressure like someone's hand pressed gently to his heart. He'd taken Leo for granted knowing, the way a shadow falls when you block the sun, that he was there around him, inside him: blood, air, salt, brain, soul. They were genetic duplicates, twins, spiritual halves. Without him, Zack knew the first icy tugs of panic.

From the Author:
http://www.eyescry.com/html/publications.htm

On Amazon:
http://www.amazon.com/Pale-Zenith-Wendy-Rathbone-ebook/dp/B00DRHMB00/

The Foundling
by Wendy Rathbone

Diego is a powerful man with a tragic past. Out on the expansive ocean in his private yacht, he discovers a beautiful and mysterious man adrift on a raft, near death. The bond that forms between them in the aftermath of Alec's rescue is one of fierce passion, though lacking in trust. Can they make it work, or will Alec's amnesia bring forth secrets so disturbing as to tear them apart? A passionately erotic love story of desire and darkness, exquisite and explicit.

I can see his struggle between gratitude and uneasiness. He is buffeted by all things new and strange. He does not know where he is from, who he is or what happened to him. He does not know me. There has not been enough time to transition between strangers and friendship.

This isolation of his is something I can identify with, but it is also a feeling no one can help him with until or unless he gets his own life back. And his memory.

If that doesn't happen, then it will take time for him to build a new life. He is polite to me, even friendly, but even a night together during a storm with his arms wrapped tight around my waist doesn't calm the surge I see inside him, the emptiness, the loss, possibly even panic. That night may have reinforced some trust in me, but so far not enough for him to completely relax.

He seeks me out, though. That's something. He sits by me at dinner when he can have any seat of his choosing. I watch him closely when he does not realize it. At dinner the following night after we had only 'slept' together, and before we go to bed again in separate rooms, I notice everything about him, how he moves, the way the air warms when he is closer to me, the dry sheen of his lips as they part for more air when he is reacting to something, or speaking, or eating.

His hands still shake. Anyone else might not notice because he keeps them clasped into fists at his sides or, while sitting, pressed tight to his lap.

I spend another fretful night alone. I dream restlessly, wild, loud and colorful visions I cannot recall at all as soon as my eyes open. All I know is the dreams leave me unfulfilled, impatient.

FROM THE AUTHOR:

www.eyescry.com/html/publications.htm

On Amazon:

http://www.amazon.com/Foundling-Wendy-Rathbone-ebook/dp/B008E97SOA/

None Can Hold the Dark
Wendy Rathbone

Now Available!
*The long-awaited sequel to **THE FOUNDLING!***

In the eagerly-awaited sequel to Wendy Rathbone's homoerotic romance "The Foundling," Diego and Alec meet new challenges in private and from the outside world. Diego is being investigated by the local police for murder. Meanwhile, Alec's amnesia and the trauma of his kidnapping by white slavers continue to plague him. And the danger to Alec is not yet over.

Distracted by their new love, both men fail to see certain threats until it is almost too late.

"Why do you keep doing this illegal business?" Now Alec's gaze turned toward him, open as the day and lit with a sad frenzy, a challenge. "You could go anywhere, do anything, be anyone."

Diego had asked himself that question on rare occasions. In truth, he got used to what he was, what he did. Even a dangerous known was perhaps preferable to the unknown. "People depend on me."

Alec shook his head, but smiled a little as he said, "That's so weak." He leaned forward, over the arm of the chair, and put his shaking hand on the back of Diego's head. The kiss was cool, lingering, moist with salt. When Alec pulled back, he said almost matter of factly, "It's like there's sharks and there's goldfish and one can't decide to become the other."

Diego was still stunned by the kiss. But the words hit him hard. In them was the unfair conjecture of a locked fate. He believed in making his own fate...or luck. Did Alec think only one kind of man lived inside him and that was all there was to it? To life? It hurt. Badly.

Diego sat back on his heels, catching himself with his hands on the smooth, plank floor. "So, Alec, which am I?"

Alec frowned.

Diego said, "I made choices in my life. I made them No one made them for me. If I need to be strong I'm strong. If I need to be vicious I can be that too. So what? I'm stuck there? In a pattern, a role...with no free will?"

Alec watched him inquisitively now.

"Because," Diego went on, "I'm solely responsible for my actions. Me. Could you say the same of the shark?"

They both waited, the silence covering them in muggy discomfort.

"You think you understand me?" Diego finally asked.

http://www.amazon.com/None-Hold-Dark-Wendy-Rathbone-ebook/dp/B00G3OCYZ6/

My House Is Full of Whispers
Wendy Rathbone

Ten erotica short stories by Wendy Rathbone - former winner of the prestigious WRITERS OF THE FUTURE contest!

Leda has not one beautiful man, but two. Kale enters a secret world in a wealthy man's basement. Noah is in love with a man who hates sex. Dina lives next door to a famous Hollywood director she secretly loves. Dorian has a sixteen year old female student coming onto him. Tara is haunted by an erotic ghost. Young Dimitri is kidnapped by lecherous men. And more.

Author's Preface

When I wrote these stories, I deliberately set out to gently break down certain barriers, and I've certainly broken taboos. Do I care? No. This is fantasy at its purest level. The stories are never meant to be political statements, nor do they make any attempt at political correctness, and there is little consideration for safe sex. While I definitely condone safe sex, my stories come from fictional realities in my head where safe sex is not much of a concern because, well, it's imaginary and it's fiction!

For me, these stories are meant as little poetic erotic ramblings merely to stir the flames of desire, nothing more. They are pure fantasy and therefore to be enjoyed as such. Every story is erotic in nature, meant to titillate, some more explicit than others. Some of the stories are light, some are darker. I invite the reader to a feast of diversity and delight.

One reader commented: "...some of the most beautifully written erotica since Anais Nin!"

From the author: www.eyescry.com/html/publications.htm
On Amazon: http://www.amazon.com/House-Full-Whispers-Wendy-Rathbone-ebook/dp/B00IJK3G04/

UNEARTHLY
by Wendy Rathbone

A Collection of
Award-Winning Poetry

Intro by the Author: This book contains all my out of print chapbooks (mini-collections of an author's work usually published by smaller presses.)

The chapbooks published within include:
Moon Canoes, published by Dark Regions Press, 1994
(Im)mortal, published by Shadowfire Press, 1996
Scrying The River Styx, published by Anamnesis Press, 1999
Autumn Phantoms, published by Flesh and Blood Press, 2000
Dreams of Decadence Presents: Wendy Rathbone, published by DNA Publications 2002
Dancing in the Haunted Woodlands, published by Yellow Bat Review, 2003
Vampyria, published by Eye Scry Publications, 2005

She Sleeps With Vampires
She sleeps with vampires
courting velvet breaths
poem-dreams
chill-stopped hearts

Wrapped in her arms
like teddy bear thoughts
purple lips trembling
at her quiet throat
they love her more than
somber rain
more than autumn
more than ash-soft hearths of night.

From the author: www.eyescry.com/html/publications.htm
On Amazon: http://www.amazon.com/Unearthly-Wendy-Rathbone-ebook/dp/B00B0MTIZK/

COYOTE
Della Van Hise

A Novel of Love, Honor and Personal Sacrifice...

When River Willows is accused of a murder she didn't commit, her life takes a turn toward the sanctuary of a world existing at right-angles to our own. Combining the mysticism of martial arts and the romantic conflict of a young woman torn between two powerful men, COYOTE takes the reader on an epic journey of dangerous secrets, military cover-ups, and the infinite heart of the peaceful warrior.

"So who's Coyote?" I asked, trying to ignore the effect he was having on me. "You?"

Steale laughed easily, though it did little to hide the torment behind that mask of indifference he wore so well.

"Coyote's a scavenger, Jack of all trades. The Native Americans call him the trickster - the one who brought chaos down on the world." He shrugged as if altogether unconcerned. "Original sin."

"Is that what you are?" I asked, keeping it light despite the growing knot my stomach. "Original sin?"

He kept his profile to me, eyes straight ahead as he drove. "Sure you want to know?"

I couldn't help wondering if I had cornered the coyote, or if the clever trickster had cornered me.

By the author of **KILLING TIME** – without a doubt the most controversial **STAR TREK** novel ever published!
From the Author: www.eyescry.com/html/publications.htm
On Amazon: http://www.amazon.com/Coyote-Della-Van-Hise-ebook/dp/B00DRNEINC/

SONS OF NEVERLAND
an erotic vampyre novel by
Della Van Hise

"The virtuosity shown here is only the beginning of a pyrotechnic talent unfolding into the hidden dimensions of the human and nonhuman spirit."

-Jacqueline Lichtenberg

"Sensual! Sexy! Surreal!"
-North County Times

"A literary triumph where the undead have more heart & soul than the living."
-The Readers

"What Sons of Neverland resembled to me was the creative hagiographies of Nikos Kazantzakis, where a few stylized characters deliver a message that goes way beyond the parameter of the characters themselves. And much like Kazantzakis, this book zones on the question of immortality. However, this is not just the decadent historical immortality of the long-lived vampire, it is immortality as a change in one's perception. This is the story behind the story, delivered by characters that are hyper-real - each one loaded with symbolism. Sons of Neverland will have you filled, even brimming over with the sense of Mysterium Tremendum et Fascinans. Go there for a full helping of the numinous." (A Reviewer on Amazon!)

Set against a backdrop of contemporary culture, SONS OF NEVERLAND explores the universal questions of life & death, sex & love - the most crucial challenges every human being faces - through the eyes of the immortal vampire.

Readers have compared SONS OF NEVERLAND to the works of Anne Rice, Carlos Castaneda, and Anais Nin. One reader summed it up as follows: "SONS OF NEVERLAND is one of the most erotic books I've ever read. I found it totally uplifting regardless of the gritty story In the end, it made me realize that light can't exist without darkness. Thank you for a truly exceptional read!" (Charlene J.)

A shorter version of this book was published in TOMORROW MAGAZINE, under the title "Kiss of the Black Angel." The novel in its entirety was published as a limited first edition under the title "Ragged Angels."

YEAR OF THE RAM
Della Van Hise

Year of the Ram was described by one reviewer as... "A spacefaring gay romance full of love, angst, and longing."

Only after Star Commander Morgan Diego becomes an exile as a result of a Galaxy Corps political blunder does he begin to realize how much he valued the companionship of his second in command - the mysterious Lucien, an Alfarian who is more elven than human, with peculiar powers & abilities which begin to unfold as he, too, realizes what he has lost.

Separated by circumstance from his former life, Morgan is thrust into a world where he must survive by his wits. When he meets a peculiar little old man calling himself Kim Le, Morgan finds himself in a situation where he is required to master The Art - not only a form of human & extraterrestrial martial arts, but a way of living and being that will alter his life forever.

At the temple, he is introduced to his new teacher, another Alfarian who begins to steal his heart - a heart which is already promised to Lucien. Torn and conflicted, Morgan struggles with the world he left behind and the world he now inhabits.

Beginning to believe he may never again return to his ship and to the friends and loved ones he left behind, he is all the more frustrated and heartbroken when a new Master arrives at the temple: a man to whom Morgan is immediately drawn both mentally and physically, a man who is strikingly familiar... yet utterly alien.

Year of the Ram is a fully-fleshed novel, approximately 97000 words, with a focus on the love story and romance angle. Set against a science fiction milieu, it explores the infinite possibilities of the human and alien heart. Sexual content is explicit, though is not the primary focus of the novel.

For those who like a romance that forces its characters to contemplate the ecstasies AND the agonies of love... you will enjoy *Year of the Ram* immensely.

From the Author:
http://www.eyescry.com/html/publications.htm

On Amazon:
http://www.amazon.com/Year-Ram-Della-Van-Hise-ebook/dp/B003YOSCKO/

TEACHINGS OF THE IMMORTALS
by Mikal Nyght
So... You Want To Live Forever?
The teachings are presented as brief vignettes in no particular order of importance. This is not a book you read from start to finish in a single night. It s a grimoire of self-creation, intended to be contemplated slowly so as to be assimilated wholly. Pick it up and turn to a page at random. Where your eyes come to rest on the page is your lesson for the day. Go no further until you have assimilated the lesson totally.

The teachings are seduction as much as instruction. This is the way of The Dark Evolution.

Two Brief Excerpts...

The Ruby Slippers
The danger of the consensual continuum is that its natural gravity exists at the lowest common denominator of human experience, and because of this it will automatically make you forget those elusive truths you've fought to learn, and before you know it you're lost in petty dramas again, sinking into the mire of old familiar scripts.

The only way to overcome this is to be continually cavorting with worlds and events beyond human experience, journeying into the unknown so that it can become known, expanding knowledge and awareness to become more than you were, bringing back from the Dreaming those secrets which will teach you how to use the ruby slippers to transport yourself over the rainbow to the vampyre wizard's secret lair.

Perception
This is the nature of reality: to be precisely what perception dictates, as solid and whole as your interpretation of it, or as changeable and eternal as you permit it to be.

It wasn't knowledge god tried to keep from Man, you see. It was perception, for perception alone has the power to destroy god and obliterate comfortable consensual realities to create unending immortality.

Take the apple, my embryonic children. Nibble its red red flesh. Open your vampyre eyes so you may finally begin to See.

From the Author: www.immortalis-animus.com
On Amazon: http://www.amazon.com/Teachings-Immortals-Mikal-Nyght-ebook/dp/B00C2HY5WS/

159

Eye Scry Publications
A Visionary Publishing Company
www.eyescry.com/html/publications.htm

www.ingramcontent.com/pod-product-compliance
Lightning Source LLC
Chambersburg PA
CBHW032213190626
46810CB00019B/3045